SUBLIMINAL

SUBLIMINAL

C.B. BARRIE

ROBERT HALE

First published in 2017 by Robert Hale, an imprint of
The Crowood Press Ltd, Ramsbury, Marlborough
Wiltshire SN8 2HR

www.crowood.com

British Library Cataloguing-in-Publication Data
A catalogue record for this book is available from the
British Library.

ISBN 978 0 7198 2377 0

Typeset by Jean Cussons Typesetting, Diss, Norfolk

Printed and bound in India by Replika Press Pvt Ltd

Chapter 1

Emma Lilton paused as she came up to the research director's smooth, grey, unglazed office door.

She held back giving notice of her arrival while she steeled herself for what was to come. As far as she knew, none of the other senior programme managers had been 'invited' to see the director, so it was odds-on that she had been singled out for something exceptional or unpleasant.

What it was she could not even begin to guess, but presumed she should resign herself to bad news. The invitation was, if the rumours were right, ominous.

Only once before had she been privileged with a personal interview with the director, and that was to tell her that she had been promoted to the management of the behavioural sciences unit – a poison chalice according to her predecessor, who had quit over the director's third refusal to allow him leave to attend a major conference on advances in psychology.

Rumours had been flying about the centre for a few days now and most of the senior research staff were anticipating something dire. As usual the paranoia was creating a tense if not belligerent atmosphere, with various research teams suffering mutually destructive squabbles as the tension escalated. First on the list was the whispered belief that several major projects were to be scrapped and staff to be made redundant. Second in line was the expectation that the whole complex was to be either sold off or shut down. Either way, if correct, people were for the chop.

As a result, most of the centre's research programmes had effectively ground to a halt as lethargy and futility set in.

Emma decided – regardless of the outcome – that she was going to retain her dignity. She had fought her way up to her present seniority against worse odds than she might face now; indeed, she was proud of her research record and her standing. The director wasn't going to be allowed to humble or demoralize her. At worse she might be looking for another job but, if that were the outcome, it would be an active and determined search. She was good, very good, and no one could say otherwise. Her PhD at UCL in autistic perception had been acclaimed as outstanding by her examiners during her viva voce. But the downside of working for seven years outside of academia in a commercial research operation was the lack of academic and research credibility. She had been immersed in business inaugurated research under strict confidentiality; it meant she was prohibited from disclosure of her research outcomes other than to the client. As such, she had no opportunity to build an academic reputation by publishing research papers. In short, she was an unknown quantity. All in all, the prospect of finding herself cast adrift, for however short a time it may be, was perhaps less than comfortable. Despite her resolve, she had a lot to overcome.

She took a breath, knocked on the door and walked in.

It was a big anteroom preceding the director's main office, filled with numerous neatly positioned grey cabinets and pristine office equipment; all of it parked against walls decorated with a pastel green emulsion and liberally sprinkled with bright prints of abstract paintings and seascapes.

The large windows were the same as in all the centre's laboratories, providing a flood of daylight which explained the rampant growth of a few potted shrubs positioned centrally on the wide, mid-height windowsills.

The director's secretary, formally dressed in another shade of grey and ensconced behind a large-screen VDU, suspended her rapid finger movements over her keyboard and lifted her head above the screen so that her eyes could identify the visitor.

'Ah, Dr Lilton, good morning, Professor Neal is expecting you – I'll tell him you're here.'

She nodded and stood by the secretary's desk as a 'Come in' came distinctly from behind the director's door in response to three sharp taps from his secretary.

She waited as the secretary vanished from view behind the half-closed door, only to see her quickly reappear, standing sideways on with her back holding the director's door open.

'Professor Neals will see you now Dr Lilton, do please come in.'

Only a few steps were needed to find herself in Neals' office; big, spacious and part library, the more book-strewn and inaccessible part was coupled to an area occupied by a large and impressive Victorian desk skewed slightly towards one corner. As before, the room was well lit by the large ubiquitous open windows, only here a set of wide, cream sunblinds shaded the top third of the window glazing.

Neals, a healthy looking fifty-year-old, neatly dressed in a pin-striped suit and sporting a clipped, almost blond beard that matched his receding hairline, motioned to a chair positioned in front of his desk.

'My dear Emma, take a seat.'

The office door shut behind her and she detected a fateful hush as Neals edged around his desk, giving a meditative pause before taking his seat.

'Well Emma, how are your research programmes developing?'

She allowed herself a moment's thought. 'We're progressing, the work on brand-name recognition is almost complete – we have some interesting results and the client should be very satisfied. The programme investigating the commercial impact of non-British, that is non-traditional food items, has terminated – again with some interesting outcomes. As for the nicotine vapour pipes, we are still getting together the range of panels we need to test preferences, but it is maturing.'

Neals nodded, apparently glad that she had kept it simple. His background was physics and he was not sure if he trusted behavioural sciences as a legitimate scientific pursuit.

He smiled, clearly finding it difficult to express what he had to say.

She waited, as he appeared to compose himself.

'Emma, I'm sorry but I have some bad news and I'm not going to procrastinate about it. The centre has not been running profitably for some time and a decision had to be made to concentrate on those areas where we were likely to attract new business. I'm afraid that both yours and David Woolcroft's team on sports science are to be rolled up. I know this is one hell of a blow for both of you and I deeply regret having to give you this news, but I'm afraid the executive and the board could see no other solution. That said, you have six weeks to wind up your activities, complete your final reports and hand them to me. Oh, and you will receive a severance payment equivalent to two weeks' salary for every year you have been here.'

She sat in profound dismay as Neals announced her marching orders – she thought she would be emotionally neutral, no matter the bad news, but as it came she was suddenly shaken by the reality of it.

'I take it there is no alternative – even if there was the likelihood of more research contracts?'

She was grateful that her query wasn't vocalized in a tremulous voice; somehow she kept it unemotional.

Neals gave a slight shake of his head. 'No, I'm sorry Emma but unless you know something I don't, the decision is final and irrevocable.'

For a full fifteen seconds she made no move and said nothing.

Neals too stayed mute, simply staring at her with a quizzical expression.

Still silent, she got up from her chair and turned towards the door. As the office door opened, Neals' voice wafted towards her. 'Emma, please remember – you will need to sign the requisite composite non-disclosure agreement before you go. Oh, and I'm very happy to give you a reference, just drop me a note reminding me.'

She half turned towards Neals and with a look of disdain shut his office door behind her. For a brief moment a surge of anger filled her, but then she let it go and turned her thinking towards survival. That was paramount.

'Trust all is well, Dr Lilton?' the secretary queried.

'No – it bloody isn't,' she replied.

Chapter 2

S HE SIGNED THE job application form with a flourish, though there was no confidence implicit in the signature.

This was the thirty-third snail-mail or email job application she had completed in the last four months and so far there had been almost as many rejections. At first, as each post or email response had arrived her spirits had lifted, but now she was resigned to the fact that every email or letter she opened would politely decline her services. This was invariably followed by a flash of anger, a sense of despair and then the trawling of her stoicism for yet more endurance. As she surveyed her paper-swamped desk, and her now untidy, well lived-in apartment, it became clear that her prospects were becoming less promising by the day. Every possible recruitment opportunity, via scientific journals, technical publications or the science-based internet websites, had been scrutinized in search of a position for which a woman with her qualifications and experience could potentially be shortlisted for an interview.

But it hadn't happened.

Not surprising, she mused, the universities had already completed most of their recruitment for academic and research posts, and there were too few commercial research establishments likely to be looking for new staff – especially for someone with a background in psychology or behavioural sciences. In short, and in terms of her expertise, she was virtually unemployable. Even a private letter to her old UCL supervisor had been met with silence.

She compiled all the necessary papers for what was now the thirty-fourth application and slipped them into the big A4 envelope – checking as she did so the covering letter, her CV, Neals' reference, the official application form and a summary of her research programmes over the last seven years. That summary had been the hardest thing to compose, she was under stringent non-disclosure agreements and knew very well what would happen if she broke confidence on the secrecy surrounding the commercial interests she had acted for. Saying enough to attract the interest of those reading her job application was one thing, being tempted to give too much away was another. Even Neals' brief reference added very little to her already weak reputation.

But what else could she do? Having no publication record her credentials were competing with applicants who had some standing in terms of published research – on the face of it she was at least three steps further down the ladder.

Her tongue moistened the adhesive strip on the envelope and she pressed it down with a strange kind of finality. This, she decided, the eleventh snail-mail application, was the last she would do – there was no time or money left for the process to go on any longer. Without an income, and one big enough to meet all her outgoings, she was in danger of losing her apartment and becoming destitute. So far her pride had made her disregard the state-based welfare she was entitled to, but now it offered an interim lifeline. A little money from Jobseeker's Allowance would provide a short breathing space. But matters had reached the stage where her options were very limited, and where finally she would, reluctantly, be forced to invoke her long-neglected contingency plan.

She thought back to the day Professor Neals had given her the bad news, the day she had given him a summary of progress in her research programmes, and had deliberately and with a fall-back contingency in mind, omitted to mention the work she and Mike Crossly, her team's number two, had been working on in secret. The timing had been opportune – the day she and her colleagues had lost their jobs was the day she and Mike became convinced that their work on subliminal imprinting was now well understood and was applicable. Indeed, evidently it worked supremely well.

She looked back at her desk. Lying under all the cuttings, discarded application letters and photocopied CVs was the thick folder containing all the research results on the subliminal work. It had been difficult to keep all their experiments out of sight of the other team members, but they had succeeded and very quickly came to realize how commercially valuable the unfolding results were likely to be. All that they had done was now a concealed treasure, a future in the making and her potential salvation. Therein lay her contingency plan, and she was going to exploit it for all it was worth.

Chapter 3

H E HAD STARTED to sweat, and that came as no surprise. The last two hours with the board of Morley, Swan & Bramly, the nation's one-time premier advertising agency, had tested his endurance almost to breaking point. He had held on to his temper for the whole of the grilling they had instigated, and had maintained his dignity and self-assurance against every insinuation, accusation and expression of distrust thrown at him. Even when he had been charged with incompetence he'd refrained from forcefully reminding them of how dire things had been with the agency's balance sheet when he had first been appointed as CEO. But so much for his past record!

He had been in charge of MS&B for the last two years and up until six months ago had overseen a 35 per cent increase in earnings with a commensurate improvement in profits. Almost single-handedly he had won, and secured, some very big commissions from major corporate interests and had at times literally ripped the contracts out of the hands of his competitors. He'd offered guarantees about improved turnover and sales, had promised more TV airtime for the same fee they had paid in the past and had assured them of a broader cultural message. Similarly, an advertising campaign that would not only be innovative and grip the viewers' attention, but more importantly, endear the brand to the viewer.

It was he who had set up an independent video production company tied directly to the agency. Likewise, he had initiated a purge of unwanted and poorly contributing staff and had seen them replaced with highly motivated and supremely imaginative people. Oh yes! It had transformed the way the agency worked, and had given them a competitive edge and a quality in their advertising campaigns that made all the other agencies envious of a success they could only dream of. His clients were ecstatic as their sales levels almost doubled and their product competition floundered.

But the honeymoon period had ended.

What he had done, his competitors had eventually done too, bringing in new blood and new ideas. They had even hijacked his own people, making them offers they couldn't refuse. Slowly, his advantage had been eroded and now he was faced with a dilemma he thought would never occur; he was back to square one, back to the situation he was in two years previously – only this time he didn't have an immediate answer to the dilemma. He had to think again.

For Emma Lilton it had required very little in the way of research – the internet had thrown up at least ten major advertising agencies in the UK and she had started seeking access to the top ten the moment she had either an email address or a telephone number. In nearly all cases she had both, but when trying a telephone call first, she found it difficult to break down the barrier between herself and the senior manager's secretary. Too often she was told that her request for an interview would be conveyed to the individual in question and an answer would be forthcoming.

'When?' she would ask.

'As soon as possible' or 'When he returns' was invariably the reply.

And so it went on, the same kind of reply time after time.

It was only when she dialled the number of Morley, Swan & Bramly that she struck gold.

A soft, well-modulated male voice answered as the ring tone ended.

'Morley, Swan and Bramly – who's speaking?'

She felt her heart lift.

'Good morning, my name is Dr Emma Lilton, may I ask to be put through to your managing director?'

There was a slight pause before the voice said, 'Are you sure you want this office? This is the CEO's office. If you wish to report a medical problem you need to contact our personnel office, if you hang on I'll transfer you to their num....'

'No – I'm not a doctor of medicine. I'm a behavioural scientist – this enquiry has nothing to do with anything medical – I may have some interesting research results that could advantage your advertising campaigns. But I need to talk to the right person on your staff – someone who can make decisions.'

She again experienced a brief silence at the end of the phone, then the voice replied, 'My name is Jonathan Woodbridge, I'm CEO here, will I do?'

The offices were in central London in Fleet Street, further down and across the street from the law courts. As she stood outside looking up at the recently cleaned Victorian façade of the building, the old brickwork now mingled with reproduction period double-glazing. Though converted to an office complex, it had been tastefully done.

As she stood her ground, throngs of people hurried past and around her, on their way to what she imagined were far more interesting occupations than hers. It occurred to her that maybe, just maybe, it had been a mistake to pursue a scientific career. Perhaps she would have been more successful sticking to something more mundane and more lucrative with less chance of being isolated and redundant. She was a specialist with too limited an expertise to be useful in any other area except her own narrow field. As she hesitantly entered through the swing doors into the foyer she remembered the old curse about specialists – they were *people who knew more and more about less and less and ended by knowing absolutely everything about nothing*!

Morley, Swan & Bramly were on the third floor – a plush open-plan set of offices and spaces with private areas set apart by off-white screens and partitions.

Finding the receptionist was not easy and when at last she was shown the office door of Jonathan Woodbridge's secretary, she had encountered at least five of the agency's staff, all of whom had been enormously helpful and sympathetic to her plight. Of the receptionist, or the CEO's secretary, there was no sign but she had acquired a cup of coffee in her travels, had seen a paste-up for a new advertisement to promote a lipstick, had been offered a free sample of a new toffee bar and been introduced to the latest bundle of joy born to one of the female staff. Given her social isolation over the previous four months, by the time she arrived at Woodbridge's secretary's door she felt as if she was suffering from sensory overload.

One of the staff that had helpfully given her the guided tour opened the secretary's door and suggested she take a seat until either one or the other of the absent bodies appeared. As she entered, almost simultaneously a door at the far side of the office opened and a young woman, attractively dressed and perfectly made up, came out carrying a sheaf of papers. She looked preoccupied and was a few strides into the office before she noticed there was someone waiting for her.

'Oh – I'm sorry, I'm Emma Lilton, I believe I have an appointment with Mr Woodbridge.'

The secretary gave a brief smile and immediately turned around and gave a knock on the door behind her. Still trying to avoid spilling all the papers she was carrying, she bent forward as she opened the door with her free hand and said, 'Dr Lilton's here – you were expecting her.' Emma waited as the far door remained open but nothing vocal indicating an invitation escaped the open door. Then the secretary nodded her head and pushed the door back, at the same time turning to Emma and indicating by flapping her free hand that Emma should enter the far room. Given her recent experience, and less than convinced of what she might expect, Emma did as she was bid.

The office she walked into was reasonably spacious but had a sense of order about it. The ubiquitous desk was directly in front of her as she entered. Up against one wall was a large bookcase fronted by a leather suite, forming a ring of seats around a circular coffee table. Here and there were small tables carrying odd pieces of office equipment – a table-top photocopier in one corner, a printer too, what appeared to be a drinks cabinet in another. The windows were smaller than she had become accustomed to, but the lighting was more than adequate.

As for Jonathan Woodbridge, she was surprised and impressed.

He stood at least six foot tall and had a slim, athletic look. He was dressed in a light blue, well-tailored suit which complemented his shirt and tie perfectly. His dark hair matched an olive complexion and he gave a very genuine and pleasing smile as she looked at him. He came towards her, his hand outstretched for a handshake. 'Dr Lilton I presume, I'm very pleased to meet you.'

Chapter 4

Emma Lilton was far from diminutive and although dressed formally with a severe hairstyle, she had a very feminine and attractive appearance. There was nothing nervous about her movements or her smile, which when he shook hands with her was assured, genuine and to him engaging. He greeted her in his usual manner.

'Well, so glad to meet you at last Dr Lilton. I trust you've had the mandatory tour – we make it a rule that any visitor looking slightly lost gets the full treatment. Somewhat sycophantic and mercenary I'm afraid but then, to my staff, you might be a potential client! Bottom line… we are a business and we don't miss an opportunity to impress where we can and get new commissions. Now, please – have a seat.'

He turned and proffered one of the leather-backed chairs arrayed in front of his desk. As she moved forward he opened his office door and took the eye of his secretary. 'Margaret, I'm busy for the next hour, no interruptions please!'

He made his way back to his desk, sank into his executive chair and once again took stock of his visitor. She didn't look insane, but then, too many times people he had met in his office offering a foolproof way of increasing turnover had lost sight of reality or were outrageously unpragmatic. Which way would this one go?

'Well Dr Lilton, you got my attention when we spoke on Monday but I was left with a feeling that what you promised me was going to be very hard to deliver. Believe it or not, I've had any number of people sitting where you are today giving me an absolute assurance that they had a scheme able to energize our advertising beyond all previous success. Never – and I say again, never – has any one of them disclosed an approach that could or would work. That being the case you will forgive me if I tend to appear sceptical when new ideas are thrown at me. Now, on the basis that this is a fresh start, shall we begin?'

He was surprised when she made no comment but simply lifted herself out of her chair and dropped a thick wad of stapled papers on to his desk. It had been orientated so that as he looked down at the top sheet he saw a printed heading; it read 'Confidentiality Agreement'.

She sat back in her chair. 'I can't disclose anything to you today unless it is under a non-disclosure agreement like the one before you. You can of course have it checked by your legal representatives but it's quite conventional – it simply means that what we discuss today is not to be divulged to anyone else at any time – not even your principals, colleagues, friends, wife or lover.'

He was briefly taken aback; for once he was in the company of someone that had a sensible business approach – and for the moment it threw him. If she wanted to negotiate under a confidentiality screen it could be that she really believed she had something valuable to tell him. If so, there was nothing stopping him agreeing to the contract. If it was valuable he would be a fool to broadcast it, if worthless there was nothing significant to disclose anyway, and the contract was futile.

That he hesitated for some time did not appear to faze his visitor; she sat with legs crossed in her chair clutching a thick folder and looking at him with lovely blue-grey eyes.

As he returned her look, she smiled. He took his pen from his inside jacket pocket, signed the last page of both agreements, and noting that no description of the confidence had been inserted in the justification, smiled with appreciation as he handed back both copies.

'OK, I'm all yours Dr Lilton, you have my undertaking to keep this meeting and its contents secret, so fire away.'

She smiled once more and took the folder she had been hugging and placed it on her lap.

'Mr Woodbridge, I'm sure I'm an unknown quantity as far as you are concerned and I expect you to find what I am about to say implausible, but I assure you I can prove what I claim. First things first. I am, as I told you, a behavioural scientist; my work over the last seven years following on from my PhD has been with the Longmore Research Establishment located near Ashdown in Kent. We are – we were I should say – a multidisciplinary research operation taking on commissions from a wide range of corporate interests. I spent the last seven years as head of the psychology and behavioural sciences group. I won't bore you with all that we did, and in any case I am myself prohibited by a composite non-disclosure agreement from telling you about it, but when I left the establishment I had just completed a research programme that has no restriction on disclosure and has no ties to any commercial interest belonging to Longmore or anybody else. The research I'm going to tell you about was done initially as a fascinating sideline. If the truth be told, the subject matter has interested me since my undergraduate days. With the assistance of one of my colleagues I investigated this subject intermittently over eighteen months carrying out a range of what were, in effect, secret experiments. I have here the results of those experiments and, if you still have the inclination, I would like to tell you about them.'

He sat back further in his chair. She spoke authoritatively and in a way that made him want to know more – so, why not?

'You seem to have your head screwed on, Dr Lilton. The agreement I just signed demonstrates that. OK, as I said before, you have my full attention, please carry on.'

He watched as she settled further into her chair and opened the folder. She quickly scanned the first page in sight and looked up again.

'Have you ever heard of subliminal advertising?'

He had and the moment she said it his heart dropped. *Dear God, another useless proposal.*

'Yes... Oh yes, sadly. What's called subliminal imprinting, the insertion of visually imperceptible messages in a video programme or presentation has no benefit. I'm sorry to tell you that for all the many and several attempts to prove its efficacy, it doesn't work! And even if it did, it's illegal here in the UK and in the US. I'm sorry, Dr Lilton, but I think this terminates...'.

She leaned forward with a grim intensity. 'Hear me out, Mr Woodbridge – what I am going to tell you does work, and it works extremely well.'

She had leaned forward, almost out of her chair, now with a forceful, passionate expression.

Since he found her so very striking he was torn between keeping her with him for a little while longer and not having his valuable time wasted by a pointless proposal. *OK, another ten minutes – no more!*

'All right – go ahead, but please, don't insult my intelligence.'

She settled back in her chair again.

'What you know of subliminal advertising starts with a man called James Vicary who in New York on the twelfth of September 1957 claimed to be able to increase sales by using subliminal insertions into normal cinema and TV commercials. He called a press conference to announce that he had increased the sales of Coca-Cola by 57.7 per cent and a well-known brand of popcorn by 18.1 per cent during a cinema programme. This, he said, had been achieved by flashing the slogans "*Drink Coca-Cola*" and "*Eat More Popcorn*" at a rate too fast for conscious perception while the films ran. As far as the viewer was concerned there was no conscious viewing of the slogans – they were visually imperceptible, supposedly too fast for conscious visual retention. It's called "persistence of vision". However, Vicary had to retract his claims when the cinema manager, who had allowed Vicary to employ the subliminal insertions, told a magazine called *Motion Picture Daily* that the experiment had no significant impact on sales during the trial. Vicary eventually confessed that he had not done enough research to make the claims he did. However, the whole thing created public disquiet and subliminal advertising was made illegal – just in case someone did make it work. However, it did not stop various research groups pursuing the idea and even up until quite recently experiments have been ongoing. In 2006 a University of Utrecht group in Holland managed to produce some significant effects from subliminal imprinting but only with brands or products less well known than the ones the audience were already very familiar with. Likewise, in 2015 the BBC ran a reasonably well-controlled experiment that again demonstrated no significant statistical advantage towards subliminal advertising. In short, if subliminal advertising has any effect at all, it is marginal and too little to be of use. Excuse me...'

She paused and he could see that she was having trouble articulating her words – her mouth was drying up.

'I'm sorry, Dr Lilton, very impolite of me – let me order some tea or coffee, what would you prefer?'

'Tea if it's no problem.'

'Indeed, no problem.'

He stood and walked over to the partitioning door. He opened it and to his relief found his secretary at her desk.

'Margaret, tea for two please and very quickly if you would.'

He returned to his desk and looked again at his visitor. She appeared relaxed and except for a white handkerchief wiping her lips, there was no sign of distress.

'I see you have done your background research, Dr Lilton – I hope it is going to lead us to somewhere interesting.'

She smiled and nodded her head. 'You won't be disappointed,' she murmured through dried saliva and parched lips.

He gestured towards the partition door. 'Let's wait until the tea gets here – I'm sure you will welcome it as I would. By the way, I assume you made your way here under your own steam – please, don't forget to give me an expenses claim and your home address before you leave. We will be happy to meet your costs for today. Ah, here's Margaret – tea for two.'

He managed two cups of tea, his visitor three.

As the third cup was drunk she reopened her folder and waited for him to become attentive.

'What I have just told you about was subliminal imprinting in its usual form with the usual results. However, for a long time I felt that all past experiments missed a vital element – that it wasn't just simply persistence of vision or the insertion of the subliminal frames into the one on show. Nor the fact that two visual messages were attempting subconscious recognition simultaneously. In these respects, I concluded that the idea was fundamentally wrong! I took the view that unless there was another, better way to convey the subliminal message, or more strongly imprint the primary message, the whole idea was futile. I decided that it was direct imprinting that offered the best chance of working. How subliminal imprinting might work no one appears to have investigated, nor has anyone speculated on what physiological or psychosomatic mechanisms might come into play. However, I did, and I started with the premise that it might be akin to a form of hypnosis – not conventional hypnosis, but allied to the sleep mechanism we all have in our brains. I started looking at brainwave patterns of which there are primarily four, alpha, beta, theta and my focus, the delta brainwave. The delta wave appears during sleep and in healthy individuals tends only to appear during sleep, but it is also known as the "reaper wave" because it also appears during death, disease or degeneration of the brain – hence delta. Tumours can produce the delta wave as well as epilepsy and other disturbances. However, its sleep origin made me think it could propagate information by imparting a quasi-sleep pattern, like in a dream, so I started to experiment with delta wave references. To cut a long story short we found that we had no need to include secondary short duration messages in the main visual programme. All we had to do was to mimic a typical generic delta wave by varying the intensity of the brightness of the main visual programme. This brightness we call luminance. In every case and in every experiment we found that the main programme had far more impact and audience retention if the luminance varied at between 0.4 and 5 cycles per second – the delta wave frequency. Not every individual is susceptible but we estimate that ninety-five per cent of subjects are.

'Let me summarize – there is no need to interject short secondary messages into an advertisement. All you need to do is run a normal advertisement but vary the luminance at a rate that mimics a generic delta wave. Do that and you will get between eighty and ninety-five per cent audience retention. That will convert into a significant improvement in sales. And, by the way, it is virtually impossible to define this as conventional subliminal advertising, so it's hardly illegal. It's different, and in any case would be very hard to discover. All you need to do is to have a delta wave modulator attached to the master video luminance control, and that's it. If you wish to see all the experimental data you are welcome, I'll leave my folder with you, but it may not convince you as much as a single TV broadcast experiment. Are you willing?'

He sat bemused and amazed.

It was all very tempting – and yet dangerous territory.

'What you say is very interesting but surely the variation in this luminance that you say is crucial to the subliminal effect would be obvious – it would like watching a movie from a projector that had a faulty bulb. The flicker would stand out like a sore thumb.'

She smiled, and he could not help but think it was a lovely smile.

'No, there is no "flicker" as you call it. The video is interlaced, twenty-five frames per second for broadcast but fifty because each frame is interlaced with another. It is the interlaced frame, blending with the previous one which carries the delta modulation – the variation in luminance is virtually imperceptible, the more so because we don't use such a massive difference in brightness. The less there is the longer the imprint takes; the more there is, and the more obvious it is, the less time it takes. As long as we accept that it might take two or three showings of any given advertisement for the effect to take place the process will have the desired outcome.'

He leaned forward, overwhelmed by her assertions and suddenly enlightened by the prospect of an undetectable way of enhancing his TV advertising. If what she said was true, if what she said worked, he had once more the edge on all his competitors. Not only that, he could become so successful that he could tell his board of directors to go hang – they would never be able to whinge, whine or criticize again. And yet...

'Just a thought, Dr Lilton – but it would be a mistake to employ this technique constantly. It would be ridiculous if every advertisement we released suddenly broke all sales records. Your imprinting would have to be used sparingly at first, only with less well-known products but subject to a very big promotional campaign. That way we could simply point to the efficacy of the campaign without drawing too much attention to other factors. Do you agree?'

She nodded. 'Yes, we would have to try its effect on something not already familiar in the consumer's mind – so we can gauge the effect. Once we know how long the imprinting takes, we can use it to determine what level we need to use to ensure that no one becomes suspicious. If it's a two-month campaign, we can ensure that the imprinting is so calculated that the sales improvements take the full two months to filter through – as such, everyone will assume it is the campaign which worked. We on the other hand will know differently.'

He agreed. 'Yes, we will need to tread carefully. If I agree, how would you want to begin the first trial and who do you want to do it?'

She gave another beaming smile and leant forward in her chair.

'Once your people have composed the complete advertisement and have it on a video tape or disc, I will want it for a few days so that we can modulate the video frames with the delta frequency. You can then have it back and proceed as you normally would. You'll have to decide what product is ideal for promotion – as you say, something less well-known but well promoted. The moment the advertisement is broadcast we will keep a close eye on the reported sales and plot the improvements. It will take a certain amount of time which may not be predictable – we will need to be patient.'

He nodded his head, reflecting on the risk; the joke was that he had nothing to lose except his livelihood. As things stood Dr Lilton, the lovely Dr Lilton, was his best hope for securing his job.

'OK, what facilities do you want?'

'Just one – Mike Crossly, my old number two at Longmore. He'll have to be put on your staff for the interim. If the method works he'll have to become part of your permanent staff, if not he will not be of any use to you... and come to that, nor will I.'

He looked again at what to him was a very bright and very appealing woman. He found her charms hard to resist. The fact that he was currently engaged to his secretary made for a conflict of loyalties that he would have to resolve – but that was for later!

'For the interim I think I will have you and this Mike Crossly on a short-term contract. While you are with us, you and he collect a senior agency salary. OK?'

This time her eyes sparkled and she failed to hide a wide smile as she began to write on each of the confidentiality agreements. She handed over a copy to him with the second page visible. In the justification it read 'Subliminal Imprinting using Delta Wave Modulation'.

He folded the agreement and unlocked a desk drawer. He then placed the agreement in the drawer and carefully turned the lock. As the mechanism returned an audible click he looked up and gave her a nod of approval; she in turn gave a short tremor of triumph.

It was all going to be very exciting.

Chapter 5

MIKE CROSSLY FOUND it hard to believe his luck. Emma Lilton had phoned to say that with her, he was to begin some real-world trials of the delta wave subliminal imprinting.

When she told him what had transpired at Morley, Swan & Bramly he was astonished. It had been a close-run thing – like her, he too had been unable to secure an appropriate job and was about to sign up for a teacher training course. At least his degrees had held him in good stead and there was no doubt he would have made a capable science instructor. And yet he would have retained an abiding sense of loss; that for all his years in experimental research, having to teach would in his eyes represent a career reversal rather than a move upward.

But now his fortunes had improved immeasurably – he was to be on the staff at Morley, Swan & Bramly, and Emma and he were to pursue their earlier clandestine work through a series of TV advertisements.

His task now was to collect all his bespoke software and ancillary equipment needed to work on a video editing desk so that Emma and he could insert the delta wave luminance modulation on a pre-composed advertisement. Then would come the test – and he knew that regardless of his immediate prospects, if what they were to do did not significantly succeed, he might yet have to become a science instructor. It was an exciting and game-changing stroke of luck, and for all the potential risk, he felt elated.

Mike Crossly met Jonathan Woodbridge for the first time when he and Emma Lilton held a confidential meeting with him, ten days after Emma had given him the good news about joining Woodbridge's agency. At first, he felt a touch of trepidation. His world was the world of research scientists and their narrow culture. He not only had little experience of those in an overtly commercial sector, but also saw such people as diametrically opposite to him in their values and attitudes. To him Woodbridge was an alien species. Yet, he had to admit it, the man had a definite charm and a way of making one feel he could be trusted. There was no doubt he acted as though he had complete authority over the scheme, but regardless, he was receptive to different points of view and very willing to make decisions which accommodated all the pertinent facts.

As they sat in Woodbridge's office they were faced with one paramount decision; what product did they think would give them absolute notification that the imprinting had worked and yet allow them to point to the conventional advertising campaign as the reason for any outstanding success?

Both he and Emma were novices when it came to the relative ranking of any one product being advertised, but Woodbridge, for all their ignorance, was happy to defer to their opinion. In fact he welcomed their thoughts, pointing out that they were in a sense an ideal panel to consider the merits of one product against another.

He gave them a choice of three new products under contract to the agency: a new car shampoo, an imported soft cheese, or a European-made lager. In each case, he said, the advertisement would be animated. He showed them the draft drawings and the mock-ups for the way each product was to be promoted. Every effort was to be made to give the promotions equal TV airtime and the same length of commercial. Likewise, there was to be equal quality in the production values, ensuring that the product publicity fostered a wide dissemination amongst the target consumer. Whichever one they chose to be modified with the subliminal imprinting would be judged not only on its own merits, but also against the other two.

The decision was difficult but in the end they had a consensus, that the car shampoo offered the most problematical promotion of the three and would most easily demonstrate the subliminal effect.

Within two weeks they had a copy of the shampoo advertisement and had by that time set up the video-processing desk necessary to apply the delta modulation.

Woodbridge was given a copy of the modified car shampoo advertisement three days after they had received the original. It had been three days of worry and careful attention to the level of luminance they were to use. One reason being the commercial itself, which on first viewing was very impressive. The animation was Disney quality, the sequence of the way the dirty car became clean was very amusing and the background music, Eric Clapton's Cream playing 'Strange Brew', complemented the whole presentation perfectly. Knowing that Woodbridge had been warned that the effect would not be instantaneous, and that to avoid flicker – and therefore the chance of discovery – they would need to use a very low level of modulation, their previous experimental results became crucial.

And yet they remained unsure whether they were not being too cautious about the modulation level. By using small extracts from the commercial they modulated the video until the flicker was obvious – and then reduced it by 40 per cent. It was done in sections so that they themselves were not entirely exposed to the effect. At 20 per cent luminance it was now definitely imperceptible but was there enough delta to have the desired effect? They did not know for certain but trusted to the fact that time would tell, and that if there was no significant effect over time they could increase the modulation level at a later stage. What they could not predict was how much impact the modulation would have compared to the effect of a well-designed and very appealing commercial.

Three weeks after the modulated version of the car shampoo commercial was handed back to Woodbridge, the commercial had its first broadcast airing.

They had been given the times and the dates of its broadcast and the three were together in Woodbridge's office to await the moment. He had a fifty-inch TV monitor and DVD equipment fitted into a hidden wall panel and it was on show as the meeting convened. Some coffee and somewhat tense small talk preceded the screening of the commercial – but then it was time.

All three watched avidly as the animation started and the commercial ran its course. As the next commercial superseded theirs, Woodbridge was the first to speak. 'As before, when I screened the first few seconds here, I saw nothing untoward, no flicker and no apparent diminishing of the main picture. I know I keep repeating this query but are you sure you imposed the delta information?'

Emma Lilton gave a confident smile. 'Yes, no doubt, what we gave you on the DVD was definitely modulated. As we told you, we kept the modulation very low, it will probably take three or four viewings for it to imprint on a viewer.

We have to wait, and we have to be patient. As I mentioned when we first met, the overall effect isn't likely to be significant on the first viewing.'

Mike Crossly added more. 'And if it does work well we have more than enough modulation depth available to accelerate the imprinting. We may eventually be able to get some results with only one viewing – but we'll have to wait and see.'

Woodbridge nodded. 'Hope you're right – there's a lot riding on this. All we can do now is to watch the sales reports. There's nothing more we can do.'

Chapter 6

Jonathan Woodbridge looked at the first report of the retail sales levels of the Autoclean car shampoo and was astonished. He could have expected a 10 or 12 per cent improvement after fifteen or twenty screenings of the advertisement, just as he had seen with the Austrian soft cheese and the German lager, but a 37 per cent improvement in take-up was unprecedented. After only three weeks, sales had gone through the roof and yet the promotion was in no way complete – there was at least another four weeks of periodic screening of the commercial to go. Was it a fluke? Was it the fact that the commercial was inherently well composed, very entertaining and targeted the product extremely well?

No!

Somehow even if that were true, the best he had ever seen in terms of an improvement was a peak of 16 per cent in sales on a well-known product; a product that was already well entrenched as a consumer favourite. This whole campaign was something different and he could not shake off the feeling that Emma Lilton was going to be proved right.

Yet it wasn't prudent to be hasty in taking an over-optimistic view. Better to wait until the figures showed an undeniable indication of a positive result. Indeed, better to wait for the termination of the Autoclean advertising campaign and then compare figures. Nevertheless, his gut feeling was that it was moving inexorably in the right direction and that very soon he would be telling Emma Lilton and Mike Crossly some very good news.

When she got the phone call from Jonathan Woodbridge inviting her to an immediate meeting with him, Emma Lilton was left somewhat mystified. His tone was terse and she had the clear impression that he was either short of time or there was something amiss. When she contacted Mike Crossly, he also confirmed that he had been left perplexed by Jonathan's rather abrupt demand for an immediate discussion. They agreed that they should be prepared for a rough ride with their employer, but would in no way retreat on their conviction that what they had done for the Autoclean commercial was in no way contrary to what had been agreed.

When, a few hours later, they both entered Jonathan Woodbridge's office, they found him sitting behind his desk reading from a large sheet of green paper. It was blank on the reverse so it gave no hint of what it conveyed. He looked up briefly as they appeared and with a wave of his hand motioned them towards the chairs in front of his desk.

As they became seated he held his concentration on the green paper for a short time longer and then put it down in front of him.

'Well, good morning to you both, I trust the last five weeks has not been too boring. What have you been doing with yourselves?'

The two guests looked at each other with some disbelief. This was not the curt, discourteous Jonathan Woodbridge that had called the meeting.

However, take it as it comes!

'We have been looking at ways of deconditioning people once they are exposed to imprinting – something we thought might be necessary.'

Emma Lilton's reply implied something Woodbridge had already begun to believe.

'I take it that deconditioning would only be necessary if the imprinting was permanent and created an inescapable compulsion to go on following the imprinted message. I originally assumed, from what you told me, it wasn't, and that the imprinting would have to be reinforced for it to remain. Surely in all your experimental work you would have confirmed if it were true or not.'

'Not so!' Mike Crossly countered. 'Take our current project. If you ask us if we have seen the Autoclean TV advertisements the answer is just the once – with you! The one thing Emma and I are very careful about in all our tests and experiments is to avoid being repeatedly imprinted ourselves. Never once did we allow ourselves exposure to anything other than very small amounts of delta modulated video. It was our small panel of guinea pigs that were subject to full exposure, and they were the ones that provided confirmation of its effect. But because we only imprinted relatively harmless messages the imprinting and permanency went unnoticed.'

Woodbridge looked quizzical.

'What do you mean – relatively harmless?'

'Some were imprinted with a tendency towards a particular soap and its use – they would wash their hands more frequently than usual with a particular soap but not to the point where it was obviously compulsive.'

The remark only elicited an 'I see' from Woodbridge, who once again looked down at the green sheet in front of him.

'Well, that aside for the moment, I'm sure you'll both be interested in the sales statistics for Autoclean, after all, discounting all else, they are central to our present objectives. I have here the current and projected sales from the clients... and they are not good, not good at all.'

The atmosphere hung heavy as Woodbridge let his words strike home – his two visitors sank deeper into their seats.

He allowed the discomfort to linger for a few more strained seconds then stood up from his desk and waved the green sheet at them.

'Not good, my friends, not good – but would you settle for absolutely fabulous? Good doesn't come anywhere close to it – Autoclean has quadrupled its output. The clients are still walking around with stunned expressions on their faces. Dear Christ, this has got to be the most successful first stage promotion in the history of advertising. The commercial went viral three weeks ago after two motoring magazines featured Autoclean and endorsed it. Given that our commercial can now be viewed on the internet, modulation and all, you can see why it's taken hold. There's been nothing like it since the re-launch of the Ready Brek breakfast food in the seventies.'

Emma Lilton and Mike Crossly felt an instant reprieve and euphoria at the same time as Woodbridge announced the outcome. Emma was close to tears with relief as she realized that she had been vindicated and that Woodbridge's earlier brusque manner had merely been his way of playing with them.

As the two reached over to shake hands, Jonathan Woodbridge interjected in the celebrations.

'Just one thing – I'm glad to hear you have been investigating ways to decondition subjects, I've noticed that our underground car park is becoming full of immaculately clean cars belonging to our staff. I also hear that some staff are stockpiling large amounts of Autoclean – to the dismay of their families I suspect. I think we need to do something about it – but later! OK, time for a jolly, I think we deserve it – let's eat!'

Only hours after the Autoclean sales report had confirmed the effectiveness of the subliminal imprinting, the celebratory meal was held at the expense of Morley, Swan & Bramly; now an agency – according to Jonathan Woodbridge – poised to succeed far beyond the most optimistic expectations.

In the plush surroundings of the esteemed five-star restaurant Woodbridge had steered them to, they discussed the menu and the wine list with almost adolescent glee, each one at last choosing from the select range of dishes and giving the waiter their order. As the first bottle of wine was delivered and shared between them, Mike Crossly asked to be relieved of his curiosity.

'Jonathan, why the dour and certainly negative tone of your request for a meeting this afternoon? Emma and I thought we were about to be told some very bad news.'

Woodbridge pursed his lips and then gave a knowing smile.

'Bad vibes don't attract as much interest as good ones. I certainly wasn't going to give you the good news over the telephone. Better to assume you two are of interest to our competitors and that not all my staff are completely trustworthy. I'm damned sure it's safer to take no chances rather than trust to providence to stop anything we are doing leaking out. You'll note that now even my secretary is absent when we three meet. Our little triumvirate must remain as much an unknown quantity as possible. As I said, it's safer that way.'

As the evening wore on and the restaurant began to empty of its well-fed and pampered guests, a now well-lubricated Jonathan Woodbridge offered his two companions a future perspective.

'From our previous discussions I know you'll agree that

it's not in our interests to apply the subliminal modulation to every commercial that the agency produces. My main concern is not making it too obvious to the competition... or anyone else with an unhealthy interest... that what we are doing in our commercials is something exceptional and extraordinary. In any case, I'm targeting the big commercial campaigns that all the major corporations are interested in. For example, one Coca-Cola campaign, or say one from Heinz, brings in three times the fee compared to what we can elicit from a less well-known brand. If our recent success is anything like an indicator as to how a big campaign might go, I am confident that we are all going to be very well rewarded. That said, more good news, you are now permanently on MS and B's payroll as Vice Presidents for Advertising Strategy rather than as temporary consultants. Your salary will be triple what you are currently receiving as a monthly consultancy fee.'

They both stuttered their thanks as the enormity of the promotion hit home. But then Emma Lilton asked the central questions.

'Jonathan, what do you want Mike and I to do about the deconditioning investigation, and how will you want to modulate any of the campaigns that will come along advertising an already successful product? As you told us, big product campaigns tend to have a greater sales lift then relatively unknown ones. I assume that you will still want to outdo any past sales records using conventional advertising.'

Woodbridge paused with his wine glass midway from table to mouth, and then sank the remaining wine in one throw. He then reached for another less empty bottle on the table. As he refilled his glass he was seen, as was now his habit, to be smiling to himself. He swallowed one more glass before he spoke.

'Yeah, we need to have a deconditioning procedure – my guess is that we may well need it. I'm sure you already see the sense in that. As for the big campaigns, we will most certainly have to exceed what has gone before but not by an impossibly large amount. Again, some modulation, yes, but only a very limited amount. Perhaps we'll mix the presentation – halfway through we will withdraw a modulated version and replace it with an unmodulated copy. If we can up the sales levels by say four or five per cent, over and above that expected from a really good campaign, it will have the desired effect.'

With the future strategy mapped out, the three held up their glasses as Woodbridge offered a final toast. As their glasses clinked together, there was nothing to dilute the optimism each felt and displayed.

Emma Lilton in particular felt a surge of fulfilment, unexpected though the direction of her achievement was. To be vindicated in her science, even though only a very few were able to acknowledge it, was nevertheless a tremendous release from any sense of failure. Looking back on the misery created by all the rejected job applications she had made, she mentally spat on every academic assessor who had sneered as he'd scrutinized her CV. But now she definitely knew her worth; now she could look the rest of the world, and the bloody elitist academics, in the eye.

Woodbridge suddenly brought his glass down on to the table top with a thump and a finality that broke all their contented silences. 'Come on you two – I'll drive you home.'

Still excited, joyous and babbling, they were so cocooned by their own intimacy that they hardly noticed the long walk back to the agency's underground car park.

Emma Lilton took the passenger seat and Mike Crossly the rear. His head was spinning and he fumbled with the seat belt. The two front seats were now occupied by his two colleagues, deeply engrossed in discussing plans for the future. All he could think of was how it affected his own destiny – now was not the time for him to intercede. Instead, he closed his eyes and thankfully sank back into the softly padded seat.

As Woodbridge nosed the classic Mark 2 Jaguar 3.8 out onto the street, nothing could break the spell. It was as if the gods were smiling on them.

Chapter 7

Richard Everson disliked having to investigate traffic accidents – especially when deaths were involved – even though it was his job. He had arrived at this one well before the paramedics and the local traffic police had decided that there was nothing material they could do as far as the victims were concerned. They were waiting for permission to cut out the bodies from the remains of the car and transport them to the mortuary.

As he looked down at the floodlit scene, with the scattering of police cars, ambulances and fire engines, a small group of uniformed men were standing back from the overturned car arranging cutting equipment. He could see the wheel tracks in the grass verge leading back to the road but there was no sign of any skid marks on the road indicating hard braking. Why the car had swerved off the road so violently and uncontrollably was yet to be discovered. It had vaulted the verge and then jumped a near vertical earthen bank, ending up on its roof twenty feet below in a field. The occupants would have had a horrifying experience; but, as he knew well, people had survived worse and to find that all of them had been killed was definitely a case of very bad luck.

As he waited for the fire chief to finish supervising his men using the life cutters in order to get the bodies out, he was approached by one of the traffic police.

'Hi Richard, nasty one this.'

His new companion was Goldman, one of the county traffic cops he had come to know well.

'Hi... why is this one so nasty in particular?'

'No seat belts – none of them. Old car, no air bags fitted so there was nothing to restrain or cushion them. As far as we can judge, the rear seat passenger was flung forward and impacted the two in front. He must have struck them like a cannon ball, adding to the fact that they were already being thrown forward. From what we can see the two in front were punched through the windscreen well before the car overturned. The rear passenger's head is missing – he's still on the inside roof but the other two are half in and half out of the front windscreen... they're wrapped together in a bloody mess and hardly distinguishable as two separate people.'

Everson grimaced; the description was far too graphic for his liking and he hoped he would avoid seeing the bodies being taken out. He had only to photograph and measure up the relevant physical circumstances of the accident and then report on the likely causes. Since no other vehicle was involved, he would have to wait for the pathology and workshop report so that he could either indict or clear the victims of drink driving. Too often his reports had concluded with 'driver severely intoxicated and most likely responsible for accident'.

If his present companion was correct, it was odds-on that the first severe impact was when the car hit the brim of the bank after it mounted the verge. The car would have decelerated considerably as it struck, throwing everything inside into violent mayhem. That, he assumed, was probably when the fatalities occurred. They were almost certainly dead before the car hit the field below and overturned. He prayed that the deaths had been instantaneous – anything else was unthinkable.

It took another forty-five minutes for the cutters to separate the crumpled doors from the car and for the medics to remove the bodies. It was just getting light and he realized he could begin his survey of the scene immediately. It wouldn't take long – there was only a small area to cover and he could get his data fairly quickly.

As he took the last photograph of the car he suddenly felt a pang of regret – not for the dead passengers or driver, but for the fact that he was once again looking at the demise of a beautiful car. Now on its roof, four wheels in the air, with doors discarded, it was dented and torn and surrounded by crushed and smashed glazing. Masses of mud and grass were stuck to the bodywork, and where the doors were cut away the seats, foot wells and remaining shards of glass were saturated with blood. He refused to let it make him queasy. All in all, the Mark 2 Jaguar looked pitiful. It reminded him of a stranded beetle; one on its back and finding it impossible to right itself.

He wondered whether the Jaguar's inert mass could feel remorse. Even if it couldn't, he remained sympathetic on its behalf. It didn't deserve such an ignominious end.

As the rescue truck arrived he had almost finished his tabulation of the various distances, dimensions and track lengths, all amounting to one severely puzzling incident. He remained by the car as the two haulage men started to fix chains around it and then lay them apart ready for the powered winch to pull it up the bank. Still unable to fathom the way the evidence was mounting, he almost failed to notice one of the traffic men come up to him.

'Got IDs if it will fill in any blanks on your report sheet

– we know who the victims were. The guy who was decapitated was a Mike Crossly; the other male was one Jonathan
Woodbridge – W... o... o... d – Woodbridge. The woman
was a Dr... yeah, Dr Emma Lilton. As best as we can establish at the mo', Woodbridge headed an advertising agency.
The other two must have been acquaintances of his. OK?
Anything else... let me know.'

As he wrote down the information, the traffic man smiled
and slipped away. Now he had most of it – the accident
scene, who had died – but not precisely why. He expected
that the pathology report, or the workshop inspection of the
car, would fill in the gaps. He looked up to the top of the
bank, and as he heard the winch start up and take up slack,
the shattered car began to pull away from its landing.

There was no more he could do.

It was time to go home; for breakfast, a kiss for his wife
and then, most welcome, his bed.

Chapter 8

ELLIOT MASON ENTERED his new domain with a sense of triumph and anticipation. Against some very tough competition from senior men in other agencies, he'd become the successor to Jonathan Woodbridge.

Even he found it hard to shake off the slight sense of bewilderment as to why the selection panel had chosen him as Jonathan's successor. Even though he had once worked closely with Jonathan Woodbridge, much of his background and experience had been with Denton & Stanley, a much smaller outfit than Morley, Swan & Bramly and he had only two really successful campaigns under his belt. True, they had been iconic commercials, becoming so engrained in consumers' minds that a recent survey had thrown up the remarkable statistic that almost 90 per cent of people questioned knew the two commercials by heart. And it was undoubtedly his guidance that had made the commercials so effective – the selection panel had been impressed by his imaginative leadership and had been in a hurry to replace his erstwhile colleague. So now, only ten days after this office had been occupied by Woodbridge, he was the new owner. It appeared that the MS&B board were determined not to lose any revenue through an unfortunate occurrence.

He believed he deserved his new appointment; he was

proud of his ability to see how best to promote a product, yet he'd dared to admit that there was always a niggling sense of futility – it had to be conceit that so much creativity, resource and energy had to be expended in selling more sausages or hair shampoo to the consumer. Still, for all his cynicism and doubt, this was what he was good at, and this was what the agency was for. He intended to go on doing it.

There was only the residue of Jonathan Woodbridge's personal files and effects left in the office. Margaret Delaney, Woodbridge's secretary, had assiduously sifted through everything prior to his arrival, ensuring that anything that related to Woodbridge's private life had vanished into the hands of the family.

Margaret, an apparently saddened but efficient secretary, had greeted her new boss with a tentative but honest rundown of 'things he needed to know' – thereby arming him with a perspective on the culture of his new team. It was welcome, as was the well-prepared brief covering the entire agency's immediate programmes and commissions – what stage they were at, if they were maturing and nearing presentation to the client, or if other commissions were under negotiation. It was as he perused Margaret's brief, expanding on the current agency programmes and potential clients that he saw the phrase *'Autoclean – under CEO's management – client to be invited for debrief and agreement to proceed.'* He suddenly realized that he had been temporarily distracted by his new circumstances, and that prior to becoming a candidate for running Morley, Swan & Bramly he had set himself a priority – to establish who had led the Autoclean programme, and how and why it had become so successful. Everyone in the advertising world had recognized the massively successful Autoclean campaign. Other than the excellent presentation, no one had conclusively discovered the reason for its success. Other commercials had similar first-rate production values – yet Autoclean was unsurpassed. If MS&B could do it once, perhaps they could do it again.

Looking around his new but temporarily spartan office, he decided that there was no time to wait for the arrival and then painfully slow distribution of his personal effects from his old agency. If he was going to win, he had better start now, and that meant revealing the secret that Jonathan Woodbridge had apparently taken to the grave.

Then he had to ensure that everyone else in the agency was appraised of what their new boss saw as his principal objective; to make Morley, Swan & Bramly the nation's top advertising agency and to keep it there.

Using the intercom, he asked Margaret to come in. She entered carrying a hot mug of coffee. For the first time he took in all her features – a smart blue suit, low heeled but elegant black shoes and hair somewhat severe, but all set off against perfectly shaded and applied make-up. Her facial features were perfection and he viewed a highly attractive woman. She had all the trappings of a super-efficient secretary wedded to her job; and yet, most likely still a spinster. It was only as she approached his desk with the coffee that he realized that his last assessment was wrong. As she handed over the mug he saw the engagement and eternity rings on her left third finger, and all of them were impressively set and expensive.

'Margaret, while you're here can you update me on what happened prior to the sad loss of Jonathan? I see the Autoclean project is listed as "under CEO's management". Were you privy to anything else about the project? What about the two other people who died in the crash?'

She gave a short shake of her head. 'I'm sorry, Mr Mason, at the time Jonathan gave me express instructions not to interrupt any of the meetings he had with his consultants

– that was Dr Lilton and Mr Crossly. I was to leave and shut both office doors when he had meetings with the two of them, so I learnt virtually nothing about their activities. All I do know is that for a time they were given access to the computer graphics suite and brought in some equipment that was integrated with the video editing desk. Sam Taylor, who is responsible for all the animation work we do, told me that Jonathan gave him orders not to interfere with what they were doing and that they had priority on the video desk. He was to ensure he and his team were absent when Dr Lilton and Mr Crossly were working. I'm afraid that is all I can tell you – perhaps Sam Taylor can enlighten things a bit.'

He took a sip from his coffee and pondered on Margaret's statement. It was opening up – the consultants might be the key. At least he had their names.

'Margaret, after what you have said I'm particularly interested in the two consultants who died with Jonathan in the car crash and what they were doing for him. I take it there's no paperwork regarding the meetings, or anything that would indicate the arrangement between the three of them? What about payroll – would the accounts section have any records?'

Margaret again shook her head and raised a hand in objection; her gold encrusted finger glinting in the window light.

'I did find a confidentiality agreement and a folder in Jonathan's desk as I was clearing everything out ready for your arrival. As I recall, Dr Lilton and Jonathan signed the agreement. If it will help, I'll find it for you.'

He nodded his agreement. Anything that would start to expose the mysterious and intriguing relationship between Jonathan Woodbridge and his two accomplices might begin to satisfy his curiosity – especially if it threw light on how the Autoclean campaign had been so successful.

As his new secretary made her way to her office, he sat

looking out of the near window at the bustle of Fleet Street wondering how Jonathan Woodbridge had managed the agency; it was certain he himself could not – and would not – be the same kind of boss. And yet there was a common objective – to be outstanding and to succeed. For him to achieve success would depend on whether or not he could be an inspirational leader and re-invigorate his new staff with a will to win. To establish that, he was going to have to get a feel for all of his team heads and to ensure that what commissions were in hand were handled so successfully that the transition from Jonathan Woodbridge overseeing the agency to Elliot Mason being in charge was an invisible and seamless process.

Ideally a nice fat winning campaign to stimulate and revitalize the disheartened agency's operations would be very welcome – something like the Autoclean campaign would suffice. Not only that, it would secure his own position.

As he pondered, Margaret returned from her office holding a folder and a sheet of stapled papers. She came up to his desk with a shy smile and handed them to him. As he took it he remembered that he had to forge a good working relationship with his new secretary – so far he had nothing to complain about and he wanted to keep it that way.

'Margaret, forgive me opening wounds but I imagine you were close to Jonathan. After so many years with him his loss must have been a terrible blow. I sympathize, and hope that you and I will develop a similar relationship. I know I will find you not only an efficient and loyal secretary, but also a team member rather than just my personal assistant. In that respect I hope you will find me a reasonable and fair employer. I would like to think that in your eyes I might replace Jonathan. I also noticed your rings – and I hope I am not being too presumptive in saying I trust I might see you at your wedding.'

She smiled in gratitude but he detected a glistening of her eyes as he was speaking.

For a short while she stayed silent and then in a slightly quavering voice said, 'Thank you for that – you were not to know, nor did anyone else on the staff, but Jonathan and I were engaged. We were to be married in a few months. I wear his rings in remembrance. The inquest and funeral are yet to come but I cannot grieve silently and in isolation. It's better I work. Thank you again. I hear what you say, and I will do my best for you.'

He froze in astonishment as she spoke and found it impossible to respond. As she turned away he groped for a sympathetic and comforting reply but nothing would come. Instead, embarrassed, he looked down at the papers she had delivered and saw the heading – 'Confidentiality Agreement'. He turned the first page over and read the justification:

The parties (Dr Emma Lilton and Mr Jonathan Woodbridge, the last named acting for Morley, Swan and Bramly Inc.) wish to discuss proprietary information and knowledge currently in possession of the first party (Dr Emma Lilton) concerning developments relating to:

Subliminal Imprinting using Delta Wave Modulation.

The objectives of the discussions will be the establishment, where appropriate, of collaborative programmes of research and development and the commercial exploitation of resulting methods as appropriate, with due recognition of relative contributions by both parties.

After the type-written first paragraph, the main title appeared most likely to have been handwritten by Jonathan

Woodbridge. It had obviously been added after, or during, the time Jonathan had been briefed by Emma Lilton.

He read it – three times – each time with a sense of amazement.

He dredged up a hazy recollection from his pre-university days that the delta wave was a human brainwave. As for subliminal imprinting, he remembered it had been discredited years ago and was illegal. And yet Woodbridge and his consultants had somehow made it work – the Autoclean commercial proved it. Looking at the folder, it contained a thick mass of printed graphs and, to him, mostly unintelligible remarks and notes. But that didn't matter, it was clearly experimental data – an expert would know. So, that was it, now he had it – all he needed was an expert to tell him how it had been accomplished!

He was instantly on his feet and heading for his office door. As he burst into Margaret's office, she was seated at her desk looking at the screen of her PC.

'Margaret, contact Sam Taylor and get him into my office now. Also, contact all programme and unit heads and arrange a meeting here with me for tomorrow morning – no excuses by the way, I want everyone to attend. Oh, and if I am right, see if you can get hold of an academic, medic or psychologist that knows about brainwaves. Try all the London universities but keep the enquiry to yourself, and please stress to those you talk to that the enquiry is completely confidential. If they press you for a reason, you don't know why brainwaves are important to us but it may be to do with a commercial we are thinking about. Lastly, since you brought me the best news I've had for years, I owe you a dinner and a few hours respite – where I hope I can displace your... sorrow... with a little enjoyment. Please, don't say no.'

Chapter 9

Sam Taylor, casually dressed in an open-necked shirt, jeans and trainers, sat nervously pulling at his shirt cuffs. He knew he had to endure a face-to-face with the new CEO like all the other departmental heads, but facing the CEO was usually an ordeal to do with budgets or timescales. This time however he had met with a cordial reception and utter silence as far as the old complaints were concerned.

This time it was to do with recently past events. The new CEO wanted to know about other things.

'Sam, were you aware of the operations undertaken by the two consultants that Jonathan Woodbridge took on?'

'No, I was instructed to let them have the video editing desk at their convenience and not to interfere with what they were doing.'

Mason gave thought to the reply.

'So, you had no inkling about what they were using the video desk for?'

'Only that I once got a good look at their editing screen, showing part of the Autoclean commercial that my CGI people had just completed. I assumed that they were simply vetting the animation before it went out for broadcast.'

'You said Autoclean – it definitely was the Autoclean advertisement as televised? No chance of you being mistaken about that?'

'No – I don't think so... although I only saw the complete Autoclean commercial broadcast the once – on television that is – its first screening in fact. I seldom watch our stuff when it's televised – I've usually seen it too many times here in the agency for it to be... what shall I say... fresh? But I was very familiar with the animation, and I'm convinced it was the Autoclean commercial I saw on the video editing screen when the two new people were working. It was exactly the same as the ad my CGI group had released – no different. What little I saw them do did not involve the re-editing of the original animation. That's definite because I saw the televised version.'

Mason digested Sam Taylor's comments and realized there was only one way forward.

'Sam, get me the master copy of the Autoclean commercial, the one we use as stock. Also make me a copy, like the one the TV boys are using. As soon as you have them make sure only I take possession. Oh, and one last thing, no one is to go near, or use the video desk until I give it the all-clear – is that understood? You can lock up the whole suite if necessary but it is imperative no one starts using anything the two consultants had access to. I'll see you after all the departmental and section heads are here in my office for my introductory talk. With luck you will have something to tell me.'

'... And so to conclude, I would like to think we can continue where Jonathan Woodbridge left off. By that I mean we are top of our game and I want us to stay there. To reiterate, you can expect some changes – I may shuffle people around, we may decide on a new style to our advertising, our way of working may change in terms of the kind of product we promote. As regards business, we will go where the money is so long as it doesn't change our ethics or isn't detrimental to our status. Finally, I am instigating a product evaluation team intended to give a wider perspective, and thus a more rounded approach, to handling a campaign for any particular product or brand. From now on, the decision as to how we might handle a promotion will not be decided through an autocratic decision from this office; we will get further by amalgamating the views from more than one individual's perspective. That means a wider share of credit if we are successful, but we all crash together if we fail. OK, many thanks – I will see all heads individually later on.'

Mason watched as the throng of people who had crammed into his office began to filter out. It took a good three minutes for the office to empty and only Sam Taylor remained behind, clutching a mid-sized envelope.

'Sit yourself down Sam – what did you think of the pep-talk?'

Sam Taylor came forward and slipped into one of the chairs fronting the desk as Mason moved round to sit behind it.

'Well, I think you have reassured a lot of people, though we could do with a good few more commissions. I've only got two broadcast commercials on the go and some of the staff handling the print media advertising are getting worried. There isn't much else in the pipeline. If I may say so, our problem is that we specialize too much on the big stuff – if only we could access a wider range of jobs they would fill in while we await the more lucrative commissions. I know we see ourselves as working at the top end of advertising, but if the cake is getting smaller we had best scoop up some of the crumbs.'

It was a sensible approach and Mason had no quarrel with Taylor's point of view. Getting new orders for his teams was his job and he needed to focus on it.

'What you say makes sense, Sam. I've hardly had an opportunity to look at the current commissions to see what might be coming up. That said, I'll keep your thoughts in mind as I begin to look for new business. Now, I see from what you are carrying that you have got the videos I wanted.'

Sam Taylor stood up and handed over the envelope. It was widened by its contents and as he pulled back the flap and looked in, he could see a small video cassette and two DVDs in their cases.

'The cassette is the master and you have two copies, both broadcast quality and exactly what was broadcast at the time the Autoclean commercial went out.'

'OK, thanks Sam – I have a hunch I will need your undivided attention soon so please stand by. In the meantime I have my own focus somewhat divided; not least the delivery of my papers and effects from my previous office and a couple of speculative enquiries which could mature into a commission or two. So, if you will excuse me, you and I will reconvene once I have considered all our options. OK?'

Sam Taylor nodded and turned to leave. He then checked himself and turned back.

'Almost forgot – I found a torn piece of paper under the video editing suite as I was putting it into quarantine. Don't know if what's written on it is currently relevant, but I put it into the envelope along with the cassette and the DVDs. And you should know that there are some disquieting noises beginning to appear about the compulsive buying of Autoclean. No doubt the clients are ecstatic about their sales – but my feeling is that Jonathan Woodbridge was worried about why it was happening. Look at the paper I found – it might offer a clue.'

He immediately dug into the envelope and extracted what appeared to be a torn piece of A4 sheet. On it was typed:

Deconditioning
Proposed ways to decondition: (a) invert delta modula-
tion (b) run counter imprinting (same commercial) to negate
initial imprinting (c) Try same ad with interposed sublimi-
nal graphics acting as aversion therapy.

(b) most likely to be effective. (b) should work but
requires...

Confirm that imprinting may fade anyway depending
on...

There was no more, the torn sheet only showing what he could read immediately.

He returned the paper to the envelope and gave a nod of thanks to Taylor.

'Sam – what we have discussed today, and the contents of this envelope, would be better kept under wraps for the moment. I don't want to be misunderstood about this so I'll give it to you straight – this matter is just between us. No one else is to get wind of it and nothing is to leak out. I'm sure with your expertise you have your suspicions, but that is as far as it can go for the moment. Do I make myself clear?'

Sam Taylor nodded his head and once again turned to walk away. As he watched Taylor close the office door behind him Mason realized he was on the threshold of the answers he had long wanted. If Jonathan Woodbridge could do it, so could he!

Chapter 10

NIGEL ARMSTRONG PHD knew University College in all its political, scientific and social aspects – after all, he had graduated from the same college, researched his doctoral thesis in the same surroundings and, as a post-doctoral student, found himself as assistant to the late lamented Nobel Laureate, Professor Sir Peter Brough.

Brough, in turn, had studied in Bristol in the 1950s under the famous Dr W. Grey Walter who had begun the research that revealed the importance of human brainwaves, and had brought brain and nerve physiology and neurological research to the fore.

Armstrong always hoped that he too would emulate his predecessors, but apart from some well-received research dealing with threshold stimuli and conditioned reflexes, he was dissatisfied with his achievements. The problem was in pursuing a line of research that wasn't already at an advanced level of enquiry by some other research group. Every time he saw an intriguing research opportunity, some other group was already a long way ahead. Even his PhD students seemed to lack the kind of insight that made for fascinating and worthy research pathways. None of his laboratories were exactly humming with groundbreaking investigations.

But things had changed.

He had just completed a lecture to physiology students on brainwave patterns and cerebral electro activity, and had subsequently returned to his office, when one of the faculty secretaries knocked on his door.

'Oh, hello Mary – to what do I owe the pleasure? Don't tell me, Morgan wants me to take over his forthcoming series of lectures.'

It was his usual burden – Nigel Morgan, one of the faculty staff, had acquired the position of Professor Emeritus of Neurophysiology at Cardiff University and had fiddled an agreement with their own faculty head to visit Cardiff as and when appropriate. It was, Armstrong thought, wholly unfair because Morgan's impressive title and freedom of movement had only come about because he had friends in high places. It was a blatant case of 'not what you know but who you know' that secured him the privileged position he now enjoyed. Worse, Armstrong was the one that often had to fill in when Morgan left holes in the faculty lecturing schedule. The reverse, of course, was hardly ever true.

Mary shook her head. 'No – he's said nothing about another sojourn to Cardiff. Anyway, he's not long back. Doubt he'll be off for a while yet.'

He felt some relief; perhaps one day he could contrive to keep Morgan permanently at Cardiff – ideally with two broken legs.

'Good, so what's important today Mary? Does the Prof want an update on faculty frolics or is it yet another demand for a cut in research budgets? The way things are going the two pennies we are rubbing together will soon wear out.'

She smiled. 'No, none of those things... I don't think... but we received a telephone call from an advertising agency, asking if we had anyone expert on human brainwaves. They say that they would appreciate a return call and are prepared to pay a consultancy fee to the right individual.'

He was intrigued.

'Got the number, Mary? I'll find out what they want and hopefully take it to a cheque-signing level. If so I will ensure you get your share.'

She gave him a disparaging look and handed him a Post-it with a telephone number written on it in lurid turquoise ink. Still, the characters were clear enough and represented the potential for a more interesting life. He wondered what they might want.

'I'll hold you to your promise,' Mary said, 'though I suspect that my share, as you put it, wouldn't exactly pay off our family mortgage.'

'You never know,' he said as she closed his office door.

'You never know,' he repeated.

Nigel Armstrong decided not to delay – the sooner the better.

As the dialling tone rang out he looked forward to a worthwhile distraction – even something that simply tested his knowledge would do.

'Hello – Morley, Swan and Bramly, Margaret Delaney speaking.'

It was a very melodic voice, perhaps with an overtone of sadness.

'Good morning, I'm Doctor Nigel Armstrong at UCL, I understand you are looking for someone with an expertise in human cerebral electro activity, or if you will, brainwaves. Without being immodest about it, I believe I am one of only a few in the country with an interest in that side of neurophysiology. If you are still...'

She interrupted him.

'I'm sorry, Dr Armstrong, we have already received two enquiries from other...'

He faltered momentarily, and then pressed on.

'That's as may be, Miss Delaney, but I do assure you that whoever has responded to your request will be less qualified than I am. I studied under the two successively foremost authorities in this area – the last of whom was awarded the Nobel Prize for work in neurophysiology and cerebral activity. Tell me, have the other respondents already agreed to come forward?'

There was a short pause. 'Well, not as yet – in both cases they were to confirm their availability and forward their CV.'

He felt a slight optimism.

'Miss Delaney – may I suggest you invite me along and let me see if I can assist your firm? I am immediately available and my CV will not be required if I can answer whatever query you have. If necessary I can be with you this afternoon.'

There was another hesitation from her.

'I'll check with our CEO and come back to you in good time if he agrees. Oh, one more thing, you would have to sign a very strict confidentiality agreement. I take it you would have no objections?'

He smiled inwardly. 'No, none at all. I look forward to hearing from you.'

As he replaced the telephone receiver in its cradle, he wondered why he had not simply conceded when told that others had an interest. Because, he thought, there was the promise of what might be called a more interesting life, and the chance to really employ his knowledge. More than that, he was bored with an academic life, particularly one bereft of objectives and ambitions. He was a specialist getting older by the day, and with too little opportunity to make his specialization felt. For a moment he recalled the dictum about specialists, but quickly dismissed it. All he needed was one telephone call so that hope could spring eternal.

Nigel Armstrong stood outside the agency's offices in Fleet Street, in a line of imposing buildings further down from the law courts. As he surveyed the Victorian façade of the edifice, he was not to know that he was not the first behavioural scientist to do so. The building had been renovated recently and was clearly now an office complex. The intricate late Victorian brickwork reminded him of the Natural History Museum and there was no doubt that given its location the building housed some financially well-off firms. As such, he had no fears that he was about to talk to some third-rate outfit. And yet for the moment he remained outside, with a distinct sense of nervousness and anticipation. It was as though he was about to undergo a job interview, as though he was here for the start of a new career.

Ridiculous though his thinking was, there was yet the positive expectation that for at least one afternoon he was to experience a therapeutic distraction; indeed, for this afternoon at least, the university and the faculty administration were to be left behind. More importantly, he could temporarily forget the somewhat dismal aspects of his current research activities.

He had never seen the inside of a wholly commercial operation like an advertising agency; it was going to be a new world and a thrilling one at that.

He shook hands with Elliot Mason in his office and gratefully accepted the offer of a coffee.

His introduction to the workings of an advertising agency had been a revelation. He'd been aware of commercial promotions of course, but to see how the approach was formalized and turned into a full-scale campaign was an eye-opener. His arrival had started with Margaret Delaney chaperoning him around all the various departments; he found the tour, and her, an enjoyable and enlightening experience. She'd stood by and smiled as he'd declined a number of free gifts that accompanied some of the advertising commissions currently under development. He only succumbed when he was asked to sample a new chocolate bar 'purely to provide an impartial opinion'. It was good, very good, and he said so. As the last morsel was swallowed he was bathed in an appreciative round of applause. It was exciting – far, far better than the silence or grudging approval he received from his students after a lecture.

Armstrong had enjoyed the day and now, sitting in front of Elliot Mason, he was pleased that so far his encounter with the agency staff and the agency's boss had been a very pleasant experience. Mason had a smooth charm about him coupled to a respectful treatment of his guest. Unlike many other encounters with 'business men', most of whom had no academic background or intellectual appreciation, Mason clearly respected the standing and status of his present visitor. Armstrong, equally, quickly came to realize that Mason was sharp and highly intelligent; the more so when he learnt that Mason had an MA from Oxford.

'I'd love to know how you gravitated from an Oxford MA in history and politics to an advertising agency,' he queried.

Mason smiled. 'Just graduated and got sucked in to a political campaign two and a bit general elections ago. Had to liaise with the agency handling the campaign. I made a few suggestions as to how it should be promoted and ended up being offered a job as a visionary campaign coordinator. Started at the bottom – worked my way up.'

It was a surprise; clearly Mason had never at the outset intended to follow a career in advertising. It was strange how people upset expectations.

'OK, call me Elliot by the way, and if I may I will address

you as Nigel – we can dispense with titles and other formalities – it's less stiff. Now, before we start, I was told you had no objection to signing a non-disclosure agreement – I trust that it is still the case?'

He nodded his head. Mason would not reveal anything if he didn't.

Mason lifted some stapled sets of papers from his desk.

'Good – two copies... please sign both. You will notice that as yet the purpose of the agreement has been left blank. I'm afraid that until you put your signature to the agreements I cannot give you any idea of what it is you are contracting to. If the purpose was already printed there is always the risk that you would immediately learn what the contract was about and then refuse to sign – either that, or you could walk away from this office without committing yourself but having learned what we are interested in. You see my point.'

It was a very unusual situation, but he could see the logic of the stipulation.

As he took the two copies of the agreement, Mason also handed over a ballpoint pen and waited for him to lay the papers on the front of the desk and open them at the final sheet. Finishing each signature with a flourish, he noticed that Mason's signature was already applied, as was that of a witness – a Samuel Taylor. It was obvious that he was to be well shackled by the agreement; he simply hoped that what Mason wanted to know was going to be worth all the time and bureaucracy.

He returned both copies to Elliot Mason. He then carefully laid the borrowed pen onto the desk. That done he looked up to see Mason looking at him with an expectant slant of his head.

He smiled back, now aware that everything depended on his ability to give Mason what he wanted. He'd claimed to be an authority – now came the test.

'What do you know about subliminal imprinting?'

He gave a short gasp. What the hell was there to know?

'Very little I must admit, other than the fact that all investigations to date have been either inconclusive or negative. There is very little to indicate it has the effect expected.'

Mason nodded.

'What if I were to tell you that my deceased predecessor and his two... now late... consultants had devised a way of making it work to the point where the results were indisputable? Tell me, do you watch TV at all?'

'Yes, but not that much – I have other distractions.'

'Did you by any chance see, or hear about, the Autoclean TV commercial?'

'Rings a bell... wasn't it extremely successful? Some controversy in the newspapers about people obsessively buying it.'

'It was successful – and yes, after the campaign sales levels stayed high because it employed subliminal imprinting of some kind.'

He sat, hardly able to believe what he was hearing from Mason.

'You are telling me that they made imprinting effective? Now that you mention it, I vaguely remember one of my post-graduate students discussing it with me as a possible PhD programme. She was tempted to pursue it but discounted it in the end. My God, that was ten years ago at least. But you say subliminal imprinting of some kind – am I to understand that you don't know how they achieved it?'

Mason shook his head.

'No, not entirely, all we do know is that they used what they called delta wave modulation. It was unlike the conventional subliminal exposure – they did something special.'

He was almost struck dumb by the revelation.

'My God, if it was that successful it certainly was something special. But delta wave modulation? Now the delta wave is sometimes called the "reaper wave" – in healthy individuals it is associated with sleep patterns but also crops up when there is pathology of the brain... that is, death, disease or degeneration. Seems to me that they must have somehow found a way of using the delta wave to enhance the optical or neo-cortex so that the image or audio message is imprinted into the subconscious; possibly like a theta brainwave induced by a flicker effect from a light source. I guess it is some kind of hypnosis. Yeah, that seems reasonable. Tell me, who were these two consultants?'

Mason hesitated for a moment, not sure if it was appropriate to disclose the names.

'One of them was a Dr Emma Lilton, the other a certain Michael Crossly – does that help?'

He thought back – maybe, just maybe!

'The first may be familiar, I'll check when I get back to the university.'

Mason nodded. 'Not sure it will be of use – as I intimated, the three directly involved were all killed in a car crash, which is why we are involved in some detective work.'

He nodded sympathetically.

'Understood. So what... if anything... would you want me to do?'

Mason opened a desk drawer and withdrew a well-filled manila envelope.

'If you are still interested in this project I want you to find out exactly how the imprinting was accomplished. I can give you Emma Lilton's experimental notes, a master copy of the original Autoclean commercial, and give you access to the video-editing desk where Emma Lilton and her colleague worked on the video recording of the commercial, that was to subliminally enhance it. If, and when, you understand what was done, we can then decide what to do with it. Are you agreeable?'

My God... was he agreeable? He would have ripped Mason's hands off to get the job!

'Absolutely – never had such an interesting proposition.'

Mason smiled. 'Good, while you are working with us you will be subject to the usual consultancy fee and retainer: generous I do assure you. As, and when, we are certain of our facts and can repeat what was done previously, we will reconsider your status. OK?'

He nodded and returned a grateful smile.

Mason picked up one of the two NDAs and the desktop pen. He quickly wrote on the second page of each of them and handed one copy over.

Nigel looked down at the page now amended. Just below in the space allowed for the justification Mason had written 'Subliminal imprinting using delta wave modulation'.

He looked at the title and wondered what his colleagues would say if they knew he was chasing a subject long discredited by the scientific community. But wouldn't they be chastened to learn that it wasn't the cul-de-sac they thought it was – this was likely to be his chance for recognition – or possibly infamy. He folded the agreement and slipped it into his jacket inside pocket. Now he was committed and it caused a ripple of excitement in him.

'Just one other thing...'

He looked up; Elliot Mason had fixed him with an enquiring gaze.

'It seems that the public unease about the Autoclean campaign is legitimate – it appears that in many individuals the imprinting is slow to abate. It also looks as if the three deceased were aware that it could be, or was, a problem, and were beginning to investigate ways of negating the effect. Have a look at this piece of paper – it was found under the video-editing desk used by the previous consultants and appears to be in the hand of Dr Lilton. You will see it partially discusses possible ways to decondition those exposed to, and very susceptible to, the imprinting. If it makes sense to you I hope it helps. I think you should treat it as equally important in your work. Here, take this copy of the master video of the commercial and please, be careful with it. You can inspect and use the video-editing desk the consultants modified anytime you wish. That said, I wish you good luck – please report back to me as you make progress. In the meantime, Margaret will take you down to our finance officer and get you signed up as a consultant.'

He stood up and shook hands with his new employer, his whole mood now lifted to joyous optimism. There was no doubt – it had all turned out far more favourably than he could ever have imagined.

As he rode back to college on the London Underground he suddenly realized he was facing a problem.

How was he to keep his investigations secret? Away from prying eyes and nosey-parkers who, as usual in a closed but competitive environment like the university, would love to know what he was doing, and then blab about it. He had to keep it away from those in his own faculty; he needed to take it to someone that didn't have a vested interest in making life difficult for him. Furthermore, given the confidentiality agreement he had signed, he was responsible for ensuring that nothing about the project leaked out.

What he needed to know was how had the delta wave become associated with the commercial video? There was nothing directly pertinent in Emma Lilton's notes. What was it they had done? Who might have the expertise to find out?

The university didn't have an electronics or media studies department and thus there was no competence in video processing, but they did have a computer sciences faculty and therein, perhaps, lay his salvation. Jeffrey Innes, a staff lecturer in the computer sciences department, was known to him and had at times been a table companion on the occasions he had gone for lunch in the staff canteen. They had similar views about the management of the university and had become friendlier as each meeting in the canteen had taken place. If he was to analyse the DVD video now under his arm, then better it was done secretly in another part of the university. Yes, he needed allies, and he could do no better than to get Jeffrey Innes on his side.

Chapter 11

'HELLO.'

'Jeffrey, this is Nigel Armstrong – where are you lunching today?'

Innes' usually soft cadence remained silent for a second or two.

'In the canteen as usual, Nigel. Why, have you got an alternative?'

'No, but I want to see you later and I needed to be sure I could find you.'

'Oh, right – well if you have a few more gripes to tell me about I'll await your arrival. I should be in the canteen around about twelve fifteen.'

'Good, I'll see you then. Incidentally, try to find a table out of earshot of everyone else.'

'My God, it's that good a moan is it? I'll look forward to it. See you.'

He heard the telephone receiver go down and cut the connection. It was fortunate that Jeffrey Innes believed that the forthcoming encounter was to convey some juicy university gossip, or for him to be notified of yet more policy changes likely to disadvantage University College teaching staff. Over the years more and more administrative, teaching and pastoral demands had been imposed on the academic personnel with a concomitant reduction in the numbers being asked to do it. As such, a high level of discontent had surfaced amongst the academic body and, as yet, had in no way abated. It was the primary subject in discussions amongst staff, and rumours travelled like wildfire.

He entered the canteen to be met by the subdued hubbub of innumerable conversations and the smell of fried food coming from the serving racks and hot plates. Hungry though he was, it was of secondary importance for the moment; he needed to locate Jeffrey Innes first.

As he scanned all the tables he initially failed to identify Innes until, searching the outer edge of the available tables, he saw a raised arm and realized that Innes had chosen a remote corner adjacent to only two other tables. It was a good choice; clearly its position reduced the chances of being overheard.

He meandered through the various tables populated by throngs of prattling staff and visitors, and was quickly at Innes' table.

'Hi Nigel – see you made it. Forgive me if I stuff myself while I listen to your news, I'm somewhat peckish.'

As he took a chair and sat down he saw that Innes was demolishing a very large cheese and onion pasty, which appeared to be leaving flakes of puff pastry around his lips. Innes was well known as a junk food gourmet, his rotund waistline and facial jowls testified to his liking for body-expanding food. Fortunately, it had little influence on his well-respected intellectual abilities.

'Yeah, hello to you too, Jeffrey – are you enjoying it?'

Innes swallowed hard. 'Certainly am – missed breakfast this morning – got up late. Starving. Aren't you eating?'

'Not yet Jeffrey, I will later. For now I have a question. Do you have the expertise to analyse the digital coding on a DVD?'

Innes suddenly ceased his chewing.

'What? What's that all about?'

'I want someone with the appropriate expertise to take apart the digital modulation on a DVD – and it must be done in absolute confidence.'

Innes almost choked. 'Why on earth would you... what kind of data is on it? Not pornography is it?'

'No – it's a TV commercial, but unless I have your word not to talk about it, or let others know what's going on, I can't disclose anything else for now. Now, can you do what I am asking?'

Innes dropped the remainder of his pasty on the plate in front of him and sat back in his chair.

'No, sorry Nigel, it's not my forte I'm afraid. However, one of my students is currently running a project in video code compression and he does know what he's talking about. What you are asking, I am sure he could deliver. However, he will need to be persuaded that his available spare time could, or should, be occupied by your little project. Is there an incentive?'

Indeed there was – to get at what he wanted was worth a financial outlay, which he was sure Morley, Swan & Bramly would reimburse.

'It's worth five hundred pounds if he can do a good job and remain tight-lipped about it. No confidentiality, no money.'

Innes retrieved his virtually eaten pasty and bit in again. He munched contentedly and then, as he swallowed it down, looked up.

'His name is Simon Rogers – hang on while I finish my coffee and we will go and find him. I will make myself scarce once I introduce you to him, but if he subsequently agrees to help you then you owe me a favour. Is that fair?'

'More than fair, and if all goes well I will give you a... let's call it an honorarium... for your troubles.'

With that, Innes gave a tight smile and reached for his coffee.

The large and well-spaced computer sciences laboratory was brimming with typical computer hardware, most of it in use by students and research post-graduates. For all the analytical activity by the many bodies occupying each PC station, there was a definite hush in the room, only broken by the occasional rattle from a rapidly fingered keyboard.

They found Rogers in a three-quarter-glazed side room that had blinds half shading most of the glass on the laboratory side. As they entered he was sitting in front of three large screens, which in the semi-darkness illuminated his profile with an eerie glow. Each of the screens showed a different image – one a constantly moving series of digital bits, another an apparently wave-like graph and the third carried the image of a cube with the visible sides having different colours.

It was hard to determine Rogers' features but even with the poor light from the screens it was clear that he preferred the hippy look; his hair hung down to below his shoulders in a pony tail and there was just the glint of a gold stud protruding from an earlobe. His shirt was a crumpled, un-ironed faded check, only obvious at the shoulders where the screen light picked it up.

Rogers was so preoccupied that he made no sign of being aware that he had company, and it was only when Jeffrey Innes tapped his shoulder that he responded.

'Oh – hello Jeffrey! Sorry, I was a touch distracted. What can I do for you?'

Innes looked down at the screens. 'How goes it Simon –

any travel forward at all?'

'A touch, the redundancy sub-routine on the D to A isn't picking up all the equal signal amplitudes on the video analogue signal. I think it needs to be faster and more discriminating. I'll get there… eventually!'

Innes raised a hand in acknowledgement. 'Simon, let me introduce Nigel Armstrong, he's in the bio' sciences faculty and needs some help. I thought you might be able to lend a hand since you have a good deal of involvement with video processing.'

Rogers gave a quick shake of his head, which in the gloom of the room gave the impression of a horse whisking away flies.

Rogers then offered a hand and he shook it.

'Well, I'm far from expert but I'll do what I can. What's the problem?'

Armstrong stepped forward, closer to Rogers. 'I've got a DVD which has a recording of a TV commercial. Ideally I would like you to investigate whether there is anything unusual or unorthodox about the way it is recorded. I'm tempted to say it may well be something rather subtle. If you are able to help, what you learn must not… I repeat… must not, be disclosed to anyone else. There is a fee involved here – five hundred pounds regardless of the outcome. Are you game?'

He handed Rogers the DVD case hoping upon hope he would agree. Rogers looked closely at the case, using the screen illumination to open it. Without a word he inserted the DVD into one of three rather indistinct desktop drives.

'Well, interesting query – let's see shall we?'

Innes stepped back and turned for the door. 'OK – I'll leave you two to it, good luck.'

Armstrong shifted around slightly and gave a thankful wave to Innes. 'I'll catch up with you, Jeffrey – thank you for your discretion – give me a day or two and I'll be in touch.'

Innes waved again, shut the door, and was gone.

He looked back, noting Roger's concentration on the right hand screen.

There appeared to be three lines of data on display. A continuous stream of constant height pulses and below it a graphical representation of an equally fast moving wave-form. The third line was a graph too but here it seemed to freeze periodically, become scrambled, and then freeze again.

'I'm looking at the digital stream and the MPEG-2 encoding. That's the second line. The digital to analogue unit is then turning the digital data into a standard composite video signal – that's the one at the bottom.'

He looked again but little on the screen offered him any meaningful information.

'Sorry, Simon, I'm lost I'm afraid.'

It wasn't entirely true; he was used to seeing analogue traces from EEGs and brainwaves but this was different.

He just caught a smile on Roger's face as his fingers hit the keyboard.

'Don't worry about it – I'm going to rack up the composite signal, if the digital encoding has been played with it should show up on the video side.'

He waited as the two top traces disappeared and the lower one was suddenly magnified on the screen. The shape of the trace was constantly changing but as Simon Rogers' fingers tapped out on the keyboard, it slowed so that the change was clearly noticeable.

Rogers started to point to the picture with his forefinger.

'That's the video signal with a severe delay on its stream-ing, you will notice the peak changing in value – that's the colour picture intensity information – strictly speaking it's called the luminance; it's the picture brightness control. Front and back of the PII is the horizontal retrace and vertical synchronization signals for the picture scanning. The bit at the bottom is the "chroma" or chrominance signal – it's a modulated sub-carrier – it provides the colour information. Now, that said, there is something about this I don't understand. Hang on a second.'

Again, his fingers moved rapidly over the keyboard and the current picture vanished to be replaced by an XY graph. On it was another trace and it was a flat line but now interposed by a series of variations appearing at fixed intervals on the line.

'Hm, thought so – you see that?'

'I do, but I don't...'

'It's a modulation on the luminance signal – what's been done is to make the luminance vary over and above the normal change in brightness – a change which is at a fixed rate. As far as I can see... hold on... yes, this modulation appears to be imposed at between one and five hertz per frame. If that's double-Dutch to you it means that the picture has a variation in brightness superimposed on it that constantly varies between one and five cycles per second. If the picture were a constant white screen I suspect you would detect an almost imperceptible periodic flicker. Looking at it, it's hardly anything, about fourteen per cent – but it is there. Does it mean anything to you?'

His whole body seemed to leap at the news. So that was how they did it – an imposed five cycles per second generic delta or possibly theta wave on the picture brightness. In short, a kind of flicker effect intended to stimulate brainwaves.

Now that he knew how it was done it was essential to limit its dissemination.

'Simon – thanks. You've told me what I wanted to know.

Two things; first, I want you to keep this absolutely confidential. No one except you and me should know about it. Second – could you, if the remuneration was sufficient, replicate what was done to this video onto another?'

The head turned towards him. 'Yeah, no problem as long as it isn't illegal. By the way, what does this luminance variation signify?'

'Sign a confidentiality agreement and I'll tell you.'

'OK by me – and the five hundred still stands does it?'

He gave a short snort of approval. 'For this work, yes, for anything else we'll negotiate an improvement. Probably much more.'

Rogers cleared the screens, almost immediately retrieving his earlier images.

'Let me know when you want to take it all further – I'll be around. Oh… here… you'll want the DVD back.'

'Good, and thanks again. I'll pop in tomorrow and sign you up. See you then.'

Chapter 12

As his intercom broke into its irritating buzz, Elliot Mason was staring at the sales reports for the current batch of TV commercials and poster advertisements. They were reasonably good and he was grateful that the current success had appeared while he was in the process of reorganizing the agency. Had matters turned against him at that moment he would have endured a good few sleepless nights. As it was, he now felt much more optimistic than he had over the previous few weeks – he was getting a feel for what might reinvigorate the agency and where the deficiencies were. He had no illusions about being able to inspire the workforce, but as long as he had the vision to make a difference to what they did, and how they did it, there was a fighting chance he could make a success of it.

Pressing the intercom 'listen' key he heard Margaret's soft voice.

'Dr Armstrong has just phoned to ask if he can get in to see you today – says it's very important. I think you are free after three-thirty p.m.'

He glanced down at the open page of his diary.

'Yeah – nothing immediate after that – tell him OK.'

'Will do.'

He cancelled the open line on the intercom and reflected

on Margaret's resilience. Only a short time had passed since the terrible tragedy that had rewarded him with his job, and taken Margaret's fiancé from her. But all the sadness had come to the fore again. The inquest had convened; rapidly followed a few days later by the funeral.

The inquest verdict on the deaths of his predecessor and the two consultants would have been bad enough – to discover at the inquest that they were all unquestionably over the legal limit for drink-driving was not easy to digest. Then Margaret had had to endure the funeral of Jonathan Woodbridge, and in the absence of any other male support she had agreed to his offer to accompany her. Having succeeded Woodbridge, he too had a moral commitment to be there, but his appearance as a mark of respect was overshadowed by having to keep his new secretary from suffering complete emotional collapse. Her typically controlled, confident and slightly aloof demeanour had vanished as she had seen the coffin laid out at the crematorium. Seeing Woodbridge's distraught relatives seemingly added to her burden of sorrow. She was grief-stricken and wholly inconsolable; the more so as both families, who knew of her impending marriage to Woodbridge, had offered their commiserations and sympathy.

On the journey back home he decided that Margaret was in no fit state to return to work and handed her over to her mother for a week's recuperation. To his amazement she had arrived back at work on the morning of the second day following the funeral, acting as though she had divested herself of all her sentiment. He didn't know whether to censure her as foolhardy, or admire her for her resilience and loyalty. But then he remembered that, as she had intimated to him earlier, being at work was for her therapeutic, and removed the time to reflect on grief and despair. She had smiled gratefully as he expressed his sympathy and appreciation, saying that as far as she was concerned work was by far the best antidote to sorrow.

As he instinctively shook his head recalling Margaret's emotional tenacity, the intercom buzzed again.

'Elliot – reception have phoned to say that there is a Michael Benson wishing to see you – it's the Michael Benson; Member of Parliament.'

It threw him for a moment; politicians were hardly the usual customers for an advertising agency. It was strange territory for someone like Benson, the more so because Benson was one of a handful of MPs belonging to the extreme right wing British National Union, a party much reviled by most voters and other Members of Parliament.

Looking at his workload he was minded to refuse an immediate appointment but decided he was too intrigued and commercially embattled to refuse it. However, he held onto the open intercom line with a degree of reluctance.

'OK Margaret, get reception to bring Benson to you and arrange some coffee please.'

He heard her acknowledge and looked forward to a coffee as compensation for what was to come. He'd seen Benson on newscasts and during parliamentary debates broadcast on TV, and had little liking for his bickering attacks on the government and his clearly expressed right-wing doctrine.

He had a five-minute wait before he heard the knock on his door and Margaret entered.

'Mr Benson is here – I'll bring in the coffee in a moment.'

She turned and walked back, only to be replaced in the entrance of the door by a dark-suited man in his forties. Benson was well groomed and clean shaven. He carried himself with some dignity and even at a distance, what distinguished him was his piercing blue fish eyes; fish eyes that for some would have been emotionally disturbing.

'Mr Benson – I'm Elliot Mason, CEO – do sit down. As

you heard, I have some coffee arriving. I trust you would not refuse a cup?'

Benson gave a curt nod of his head and walked to the middle of the seats surrounding the desk.

He waited as Benson seated himself and carefully crossed his legs, squeezing the sharp creases of his trouser legs to ensure that in stretching, they would not spoil his appearance.

This, he told himself, foretold a tense meeting. If this fussy behaviour characterized Benson, he was dealing with someone pedantic and proud – better, as it was, to placate him.

He settled into his chair, looking at Benson and wondering what was to come, but waited and held his peace. Benson allowed the awkward moment to hang as he turned his head to survey the office and then looked back.

'Mr Mason, you know who I am and the party I represent. As you are undoubtedly aware a general election is in the offing; we have eleven months before the electorate go to the ballot boxes. The British National Union has decided to put up candidates in ninety-eight per cent of the seats subject to election. We are determined that unlike the last general election we will not lose because we failed to adequately convey our policies to the electorate. The analysis of the last general election campaign we fought indicates that our primary weakness was in the way our TV campaign was presented, organized and fought. We have no intention of making the same mistake again. We believe that your agency has the insight and imagination to bring our policies to the fore in such a way that convinces voters that we are the party that should be in power. Now, I need to know if the idea appeals to you and on what terms we might negotiate an agreement.'

For a moment he sat absorbing the whole concept of once again handling a political campaign. He would be in well-trodden territory on this one... but for the BNU?

'Well Mr Benson, I'm in no way averse to considering the possibility of handling your campaign but what occurs to me immediately is the cost. Bear in mind that I would have to commit virtually the whole of my operation to setting up and getting your approval for both poster advertisements and all the TV party political broadcasts and short commercials. We would have to handle the public relations side as well. I suspect it would be financially inaccessible except for those with very deep pockets – like your political competitors.'

Benson made no sign of reacting, which was a little disheartening given his attempt at irony and painting a very negative picture.

'How much is "financially inaccessible" as far as you are concerned? Give me a hard figure,' Benson rasped.

'Can't say exactly – we would have to start, and I mean start, at twenty-five million.'

It was probably seven to ten million more than needed but he had no intention of understating either the cost or the fact that his agency would be representing a much disparaged and unpopular political entity. There had to be a good reason for it to happen.

Benson paused for a moment, his head slightly bowed, and then he looked back again.

'I'm told, Mr Mason, that your agency has achieved wondrous results for some of the products you represent. I'm told, and I have read, that some of your commercial campaigns have left consumers obsessively purchasing the product in question. There have even been questions in Parliament about it – but, as yet, to no avail. Now, ideally, we would love to have a campaign along the same lines as you might do for one of your... what shall we say?... car cleaning products, or perhaps a new toothpaste, a campaign which you know will guarantee a massive lift in turnover and sales. Without getting into the minutiae or difficult territory, give me a figure for ensuring our campaign would have the maximum impact on the voters. In short, we won't be asking any questions about how you do it.'

It was a carefully composed statement, rich with circumlocution and implication. So, what was he to say? A small deception was in order.

'Mr Benson, I have only recently taken over the reigns of this agency – my late predecessor was the expert in political campaigns and I have yet to experience anything allied to that particular sector. However, that said, to me a political campaign is the same as any other product campaign. I'm sure we can meet all your expectations. But can you afford it?'

Benson shrugged. 'What are your terms – a conventional campaign at twenty-five million or a guaranteed campaign at...?'

'That I can't say as yet – but if we do take on your brief, to tweak it let us say will require a substantially greater amount than I have estimated.'

Benson smiled. 'I have access to considerably more than your first figure, Mr Mason – if you can promise to give us what we are looking for we will pay your agency forty million for the campaign and you yourself will receive an... acknowledgement let's call it, of ten million... no questions asked.'

It shook him – a direct bribe – and for what? Clearly Benson had his suspicions and it looked as if he wasn't going to be put off easily.

'You realize that if we accept your commission we will need to agree the content of your campaign; the policy message, your adherence to parliamentary democracy, your support or otherwise for various public issues and so on. Not to dissemble Mr Benson, you will not only need to win over voters who are politically hostile to your party, but not lay a trap for yourselves in saying things your opponents can undermine, criticize or humiliate you with. I recall that at the last election some of your candidates created quite a scandal with their open right-wing opinions, especially on ethnic matters.'

Benson smiled – a broad and knowing smile.

'We will not make the same mistake again, Mr Mason, with your help we will ensure we convey... what shall I say? A socially and politically acceptable set of policies. Now, will you accept my offer?'

No – he couldn't. Not yet anyway, not until Nigel Armstrong either confirmed the delta wave procedure or didn't. He needed to wait until this afternoon's appointment with Nigel to hear of progress. Perhaps after that...

'Let me have a close look at all this, Mr Benson. I need to be sure we can accommodate the extensive campaign you envisage. Why don't we get together in a couple of days? Trust me to ponder a little; I want to be sure we can give you exactly what you want.'

Benson smiled broadly again.

'Mr Mason, I recall an old adage, that administrations trust what they pay for and are suspicious of what they don't.'

There was a small chuckle of laughter from Mason as he stood up and offered his hand to Benson. As Benson came upright and returned the handshake, Mason held on to it.

'Margaret, my secretary, will arrange an appointment as you go out. Please be sure that what you offered earlier can be swiftly advanced. I might add that in the event that we agree a contract you will need to provide one third of the agency's fees in advance and the whole of the... what did we call it?... acknowledgement, at the outset. I thought you would like to know our terms and conditions before you commit.'

Benson made no sign of being embarrassed or compromised; instead he simply offered a slight bow.

'I look forward to seeing you soon, Mr Mason.'

Mason stayed standing as Benson left the office.

As the door closed he summed up his options. It all depended on Nigel Armstrong; what he learned about the subliminal imprinting was the key. On offer was more money than he had a right to expect, and yet it ran counter to his principles. But it would offer one hell of a safety net – he need never again worry about climbing the career ladder, nor endure frantic nights as the next board meeting came up.

He had to admit it; the money and what it could do for him made it obvious – that even he had his price. Ethics aside, this was one situation where everyone could be a winner: the agency staff, Armstrong, and anyone else that contributed to making the potential fifty million move from the BNU's coffers to their personal bank accounts and that of the agency. Only one thing puzzled him – where on earth did the BNU suddenly get access to so much money? It was clear that some very free and very deep pockets were promising whatever cash was needed to make the BNU's election campaign potent and viable. Still, that was a question for later. All that concerned him was making his own bank account well-stocked. He crossed his fingers – if all came to fruition he would take Margaret to dinner, and then rethink his life.

As the thought passed, the intercom came to life. He stabbed 'listen' once more and heard Margaret.

'I'm sorry about the absent coffee, Elliot. Apparently the canteen is short staffed. Are you still in need?'

He smiled to himself. He hadn't needed compensation for what was to come after all; the meeting had provided its own reward. He leaned towards the intercom and pressed 'out'.

'No, it's okay, Margaret. Leave it for now, I'll survive.'

And so he would!

Chapter 13

THE AFTERNOON APPOINTMENT with Elliot Mason was something to look forward to. Nigel Armstrong had persuaded Simon Rogers to accompany him, to reinforce his contention that the delta modulation on the original Autoclean commercial could be replicated at will. He knew full well that everything he hoped for was predicated and dependent on convincing Mason that they could do what he wanted them to do. Rogers would ensure that Mason would come to believe that they had indeed unravelled the mystery.

They arrived early with Simon Rogers slightly agitated at having to find his way to their meeting on an Underground system that he seldom used and was unaccustomed to. Still, he had arrived with time to spare, though his appearance, consisting of jeans, un-ironed shirt and trainers, was not likely to inspire confidence in his new master or reinforce his credibility. But it was too late for any sartorial improvements.

They waited in Mason's secretary's office, and as they killed the eight minutes before their appointment he had the chance to talk with her. To his pleasurable surprise he found her not only very attractive but also amiable and conciliatory, evidently listening to what he had to say and making intelligent replies. As she typed out notifications to current clients listing the broadcast times of their commercials and subsequent viewer responses, the intercom buzzed.

'Is Nigel Armstrong with you yet, Margaret?'

She leaned towards the intercom. 'Yes, with me now.'

'OK – send him in.'

It came as a surprise to see two bodies enter his office. Nigel Armstrong he recognized but he had a companion and it was very likely that he was probably a student. It appeared that Armstrong had found an ally.

Nigel Armstrong came forward ahead of the other man and shook hands.

'Elliot, this is Simon Rogers, there is a very good reason for him to be here as you will learn.'

Both men took chairs in front of him and gave the impression of being self-confident – there was nothing sheepish or awkward about their movements. Each sat looking up, as he remained standing.

'Good to see you Nigel, and you Simon. I'm sorry, Simon, if I appeared a little impolite when you came in, I was not expecting Nigel to be accompanied. Are you working alongside Nigel at the university?'

Rogers shook his head. 'No, I'm in computer sciences, a long way from the biosciences faculty.'

Armstrong lifted an arm, waiting to be invited to interject.

'Simon has acquired a broad knowledge of video processing – it's to do with his current PhD studies. Without him we would not be able to report anything to you today.'

He suddenly felt a sense of optimism – it sounded as if they were going to say all the things he was hoping for. He sat down and waited for a short time... please God that his expectations would be fulfilled and he was going to be right.

'OK – let's hear it.'

Nigel Armstrong proffered an open hand in Simon Rogers' direction, inviting him to speak. For a moment Rogers looked flustered and then, wriggling more upright in his seat, he composed himself.

'When Nigel asked me to look at your DVD he asked me to identify anything unusual about the way the video information had been recorded. Fortunately, I have enough equipment to analyse video signals very well – I need to for my own work.

'As we looked at the composite video on the DVD I noticed that the luminance signal that determines picture brightness had some jitter. Following this up we discovered that the luminance signal was slightly modulated. In short, the modulation was between zero and five cycles per second but at such a low modulation level that it would not be visually discernible on viewing but, so Nigel tells me, it would be enough to modulate the visual cortex. I'm not sure I know why this has any significance but I will leave that for Nigel to explain. I can tell you this, that what was done can easily be replicated on any other DVD or video recording – no problem in fact.'

As he heard Rogers speaking a thrill of triumph ran through him – so now he had arrived at exactly the same point as his predecessor and the two consultants. He now knew why, and how, the Autoclean commercial had been so successful and that it could be repeated.

As Rogers paused, Nigel Armstrong added to Rogers' statement.

'There's no doubt, Elliot, the delta wave is imposed on the luminance signal – the brightness need only vary by a very small amount. Any overt change and it becomes directly visible but if I am right, it doesn't matter that the modulation is very low, I suspect that repeated viewing of a modulated commercial simply builds up the subliminal imprinting. It takes time but with constant showing of a commercial it doesn't matter. To make the effect faster it would be necessary to increase the modulation but the more you do that, the more it might be noticeable. It seems that Emma Lilton and her colleague settled on fourteen per cent modulation and it worked well. And, as I said I would, I checked. Emma was definitely one of my post-graduate students, and my notes tell me that at the time, some ten years back, she did indeed consider subliminal work for her PhD. At the time I dissuaded her from pursuing it. I thought it was a thoroughly discredited field and I believed the same when I first met you – seems I was very wrong. Much to my chagrin, I now remember getting a letter from her asking me to notify her of any departmental vacancies. I was unable to reply with any encouragement. Sad to say, it is too late now. Yet it seems she was on to something – undoubtedly a valuable legacy.'

He could not avoid a beaming smile. All was well.

'Simon – if I may – you are no doubt aware that what you are doing in collaboration with Nigel has to stay absolutely secret. I make no bones about it so I will need you to sign a...'

Nigel Armstrong waved a hand.

'No need, Elliot – Simon is aware of the confidentiality that must be observed and he's already signed an NDA. I blanked out my signature on my agreement, photocopied every page and Simon then signed in the same place. All you have to do is either co-sign your own signature or simply leave it as it is. It's still a legally binding agreement.'

Armstrong leaned over the desk and handed him the copy of the agreement. Checking the last page, Rogers' signature was where it should be. It would do.

'Gentlemen – I can't tell you how delighted I am with your conduct and rapid determination of what Emma Lilton discovered, I think we are now well poised to take it all further. However, where we go with our knowledge of this subliminal effect will depend on a lot of factors. So… for the moment we stand back and wait for the right opportunity. In the meantime please carry on as normal until I can call on your expertise at a future point in time. While you wait I am sure you will be pleased with the generosity of this agency. I am going to give you both a two thousand pound interim bonus that I suspect will only be a taste of what I will be able to award you in the near future. Margaret will take you down to the finance office – I will authorize the payment as you leave. Please await my invitation for another meeting, soon I hope.'

He stood up signifying the end to the meeting and shook hands with both men, now tied to him by a legally binding agreement and undiluted greed. He felt no shame in admitting to himself that he was no less greedy.

As both men departed he triggered the intercom and gave Margaret his instructions. She acknowledged curtly and then switched off as the two men came abreast of her desk.

'You must have done something very valuable for Elliot – I imagine you are both very pleased with the outcome.'

Nigel Armstrong smiled with pleasure and winked at her.

'We're not absolutely sure yet – it could grow to bigger things and bigger bonuses. If it does I promise you a slap-up dinner.'

For that remark he received a broad smile and dilated pupils – possibly, just possibly, she might one day take him up on his offer. He certainly hoped so.

Simon Rogers felt the sway of the underground train as it rocketed between stations. He didn't like it. The jolting movement of the train and the claustrophobic atmosphere was too much, and to him thoroughly disturbing. It was something he could never get used to. It was all founded on his complete inability to overcome a deep trepidation when travelling.

Travelling instilled anxiety and this was psychologically disruptive. It made it impossible for him to concentrate on his usual pastime of formulating computer code in his head.

His major fear was getting off at the wrong station and finding himself confused and stranded, thereby failing miserably in his quest to get home. He had only just become confident in finding his way from his digs to the university and back again – this, after living in his bedsit for the last fourteen months. His lesser fear was that people would find out about his curious quirk, and wonder why a computer genius found it hard to navigate as easily as the average person. Nevertheless, he managed to hide his shortcomings rather well, allowing people to think that his persistently bad timekeeping was down to intellectual preoccupation. In fact it was simply down to dithering as he travelled – he was never certain that he wasn't lost.

Now, as he constantly scanned the station markings on the Tube map above his head, counting down those that were to come before his home station, he felt better for having a large cheque in his wallet. Two thousand pounds was a lot of money just to analyse a videodisc and he reflected on what might yet be on offer. Elliot Mason had impressed him with his ease and generosity, but it occurred to him that Mason was eager, if not passionate, about what the video modulation could provide. For the interim Nigel Armstrong had ignored his query about why one would want to impose a delta wave modulation on a videodisc and even on reading his agreement, which mentioned subliminal imprinting, he was still in the dark. As soon as he could, he was going to do a little research and find out more. Sadly his forte had always been the physical sciences, and as a schoolboy his parents had always encouraged his strengths, allowing him the permanent refuge of his bedroom and all the electronics necessary for him to pursue his passion. With the money he now had it was time for a short sabbatical from his PhD work. He hated the concrete, claustrophobic jungle that was London and endured it only while his studies were in process. It was time for him to return to his parents and the little Shropshire village he loved so well. There he would find familiar surroundings, familiar roads, familiar pathways and little chance of becoming marooned. With the comfort of recognizable territory he would have the freedom to organize his PhD and delve into what he was meekly getting ensnared by – and perhaps profit from it.

Nigel Armstrong left Simon Rogers at Fleet Street Underground station giving him as much in the way of directions as possible. Simon's impending trip back to UCL via Euston Square station appeared to make him tense and edgy and it may have explained his strained look when he had arrived for the interview with Elliot Mason. He had not been able to accompany Simon from UCL to Fleet Street, nor back to UCL, because he had taken the whole day off from the university to work at home through the morning up until the afternoon appointment. Not having to return to UCL at Gower Street that day meant a different route than the one Simon had to take. He had waved Simon off at the station more in hope than expectation; hopeful he would arrive at his true destination. A sense of guilt was mixed with a slight apprehension that if Simon did actually vanish, never to be seen again, all plans for the promised gratuity that Elliot Mason had intimated might well sink without trace – at least until another expert could be found. A long delay was unthinkable.

He had already mentally expended the kind of sum he

thought Elliot was considering. The £2,000 he had received was intended as the start of a nest egg that he hoped might arise and supplement his savings. A life-long bachelor, he'd been too distracted with science to be overly concerned with seeking a domestic life and had only the odd skirmish with a woman to his credit. However, Elliot Mason's secretary had kindled feelings in him that he had long suppressed. Today's encounter with her had reinforced a hormonal and psychological response he could not resist. It was clear he had to do something positive; indeed, if he was going to court Margaret Delaney, lots of money would be to his advantage.

Chapter 14

THIS TIME MICHAEL Benson was accompanied; following him was a taller man with slightly greying hair but well dressed and with a proud bearing. As Margaret closed the door, the two visitors made their way forward, the second man waiting patiently while Benson and Mason shook hands.

'Mr Mason, may I introduce Nicholas Frobisher, our party's finance officer and a member of our political council.'

Frobisher shook hands with a strong grip but his hazel eyes betrayed no sense of pleasure.

'Gentlemen, I'm pleased to see you. Take a chair.'

With both seated, he took his own chair and pretended to rapidly peruse some papers on his desk. Then without labouring the pretence he looked up and addressed his small audience.

'Gentlemen, let us dispense with formalities. I have given your proposal some thought. The campaign you envisage for the forthcoming election will occupy all of my staff for at least six, maybe seven, months. I say that because you will undoubtedly want some of it well scripted and then revised as we go along; that delays matters and we will want to start the broadcast and poster campaign a good few weeks before the election. Having studied other campaigns I am fairly convinced that a concentrated assault, just prior to polling day, will be to your advantage and—'

Benson lifted an interposing hand.

'Mr Mason – you speak of what I can only describe as a programme for a conventional campaign. We were expecting something extraordinary – as you are aware, we are prepared to pay for it.'

The interruption failed to deflect his delivery.

'Gentlemen, you mistake the tactic. Regardless of... what shall I say?... other factors, your campaign must be plausible. In other words, it must appear as though a conventional campaign has decided the increased vote in your favour. Were we to design a less than robust series of presentations, which were by any standards clearly unpersuasive and unconvincing, and yet you prevailed, we would be wide open to accusations of illegal vote fixing and underhand dealing. In short, it must appear as though any swing towards the BNU was due to policy, national interest and a manifesto that currently appeals to voters. These points must be driven home without mercy. Anything else won't do. However, that said, I can guarantee you a campaign that will have so great an impact that compared to your party's previous showings, it will be treated as a step change in British politics. Nevertheless, that is all I can promise you – a distinct and unprecedented improvement in the turnout for the BNU. If you want me to guarantee you a landslide victory, I'm afraid I can't.'

Benson looked at Nicholas Frobisher in order to gauge his reaction. When he saw him nodding his head he turned back and remained silent for a short time, dwelling on the reply.

'OK Mr Mason – we understand your point of view and we will not seek unrealistic assurances, or insist that you reveal how you are prepared to provide what you say. All we require is that the improvement is met – unqualified, outright and without exception. If we pay then you must deliver. Is that acceptable?'

He smiled, a reptile's grin, hoping it appeared genuine.

'Yes, but the terms and conditions stand – one-third of the forty million to be paid over to the agency directly as contracts are signed, and the… shall we call it a supplement?… to be paid in my name and immediately. If you agree I will get the draft contract drawn up within the week. If your legal people are happy we can start work within a month. You will have to arrange for your political advisors to spend time with us scripting your message and for your executive to sign off any of the posters and party broadcasts we create in conjunction with your people. If all this can be organized, I think we have a deal.'

He stood up implying that the meeting was terminated. Frobisher then drew an envelope from his inside jacket pocket and handed it over to him. He took it and watched as the two men stood and silently offered a handshake. He reciprocated and went to his office door to see them out.

'I'll be in touch gentlemen – give me a week.'

They left his office, and he saw them acknowledge Margaret as they passed her desk. When finally they had departed, with the outer office door closed behind them, he asked Margaret to arrange some coffee for them both, and then he shut his own office door. He opened the envelope Frobisher had given him; it was a ten-day post-dated cheque for £10 million. He scanned the cheque three times to convince himself that it was genuine. As he did so he wondered again how the BNU had managed to acquire so much financial support. It was astounding; that they were prepared to spend so much was even more astounding.

He now stood in his office, unable to conceal his immense joy; a 120 years' tax-free salary in one go. All he had to do was subliminally imprint the voters. Easy!

Sam Taylor sat in front of him with an amazed expression on his face. He'd called Sam Taylor first and subsequently Simon Rogers and Nigel Armstrong to his office to break the news about the BNU contract. Taylor clearly had premonitions about what he had to announce and seemed agitated. Before he had the chance to complete his announcement, Sam Taylor's face had started to colour up and the statement was cut short.

'For Christ's sake Elliot, I'd heard through the grapevine that members of the BNU had been up to see you. To agree to see them is bad, for us to get in to bed with them is criminal. Do you know what you are doing? The BNU are a rabid, uncompromising and bigoted clutch of near-Nazi sympathizers. I'll tell you this; if you try to get our teams to work on their election campaign you will be asking for trouble. The majority of the population detests them – not least most of our own people. How on earth are you going to get our staff to shrug their shoulders, sit down with them, and cheerfully plan an election campaign?'

He gave Taylor a pensive look. 'That's what you and the other team leaders are expected to do – persuade them. But not just from loyalty to the agency and their basic livelihood; for the duration of the campaign everyone on staff will receive an additional one month's salary every month. Not only that, at the end of our involvement with the BNU work, everyone on staff will get a two thousand pound bonus. Senior staff members and team leaders will receive five thousand pounds. And as a rider to that, I am assured that the BNU will moderate their policies and in no way promote extreme and unpalatable attitudes. We can, and will, moderate the content of the promotions we create – if we don't like it, we don't do it.'

Sam Taylor simply shook his head.

'OK Elliot, but you know that regardless of what I see as a very generous... what shall we call it?... inducement, and the agency's control of the content, some of the staff will still agitate for renouncing the contract. Let me remind you of what you said in your introductory talk, that we proceed "so long as it doesn't change our ethics or isn't detrimental to our status" and that business decisions would not flow from an "autocratic decision" emanating from this office. As I see it, you have reneged on that declaration – and it could cost you.'

He waved a hand in acknowledgement.

'Understood, but we have to be pragmatic. For the agency to survive and progress we may have to shake hands with the devil. I see this BNU agreement as a way of ensuring we all have a future. Remember, the last thing we want to risk is staff becoming redundant and the agency starting to shrink. However, that said I take your point so I will speak to everyone on the staff tomorrow. Until then, you are the only one having prior notice of this new commission. Please keep it under your hat for now. Oh, one more thing – I have two new consultants coming in to look more closely at the material you gave me a little while back. I say again – whatever your suspicions, please keep it to yourself.'

As Mason waved Sam Taylor away he knew he had a fight on his hands. It was going to be a difficult engagement if too many of his people dug their heels in and refused to be bribed or coerced into working with the BNU. For the moment he had to construct a strategy that would persuade them all that the end justified the means, and that for the sake of future security, sometimes one needed to dirty one's hands.

For now he had to attend to more mundane things, a

meeting with the CreditFirst organization, to view their new TV commercial and then to sign it off. Sam Taylor and his team had pulled out all the stops on the half animation and half live-acted commercial and he was fairly sure the CreditFirst executives would applaud what they had done. He trusted that eventually Sam Taylor could see why doing a good job for CreditFirst was no different than doing a good job for the BNU.

And yet Mason shivered slightly as he recalled the old maxim; that those convinced against their will hold to their opinions still. If Sam wasn't convinced of the more prag-matic view, and too many of his colleagues felt the same, then he was going to see his £10 million vanish. And what of his two experts? How would they react when they learned that they were to use subliminal imprinting to aid the BNU?

It was all less than he hoped for, but if he was to profit from his nefarious scheming he had to either neutralize his opponents or turn them into allies. One way or another, the latter was what he intended to do.

Chapter 15

MASON DECIDED NOT to use his office for the staff meeting; the last get-together in his office was too cramped and claustrophobic. This time the staff had gathered in the cafeteria/coffee shop that served as a refreshment area, and a calm sanctuary for when the work started to impinge on their ability to be creative. It was snug and entirely shut off from all the partitioned work areas, so that it provided the psychological break between the work environment and a place separate from any immediate pressure.

As he waited, he expected the same level of commotion and uproar as he had experienced before and after his earlier introductory talk. But this time they filed in and stood quietly; a sullen and resentful quiet that had ominous overtones. His guess was that no matter the undertaking of those in the know to keep private the negotiations with the BNU, it was unavoidable that rumours would spread and infect the whole team.

As it was clear that nearly all the forty-eight members of staff had appeared, Mason stood up on the safety platform. Even so, it felt slightly slippery and unstable; not surprising since it had been commandeered from behind the food and refreshments counter to heighten some of the shorter kitchen staff as they served.

Once sure of his footing he swung his gaze over the assembled employees, realizing that he had yet to meet all of them personally, and that for all the weeks he had been in office too few had ever seen him on a face-to-face basis. But the trick was to turn a disadvantage into an advantage. From a strategic point of view, it was all to the good.

He took a breath and started his introduction.

'Good morning everyone. Again, let me apologize to all of you that have not, as yet, had a chance to meet me in person and submit the odd gripe or two. It will happen, I promise. One of the reasons that it hasn't happened so far is that from the moment I took over here I have been pretty well tied up with one very important issue. That issue is the future of the agency and the job security of everyone here. I'm sure you are all aware that under the management of my predecessor Jonathan Woodbridge the agency was beginning to limp along. Yes, surviving it was, but for an agency with such an impeccable pedigree it was all very unsatisfactory. I was appointed to do something about this lapse in our success and it is to be admitted that some of the credit I might now take is for projects that were instigated by Jonathan. As you know, the Autoclean campaign he oversaw was immensely successful. It is sad that he was never to know the full extent of that success. I want us to sustain his legacy and the excellence of our work, and to ensure we are not reduced to becoming a second-rate has-been, forcing us to subsist on low-budget commissions. I am determined that we will continue to guarantee our future job security and our attractiveness to external commissions. I take it as a natural consequence of the reputation this agency has that we are the first port of call for any corporation, firm or organization that wants to begin a first-rate advertising campaign, and for it to be anathema for any existing client to think about deserting us for another agency. To this end,

I have recently discussed with, and contracted with, the British National Union to handle the whole of their pre-election advertising campaign. I want it understood that...'

He suddenly heard a commotion at the back of the crowded throng and a woman pushed through to the front. She was obviously nervous but she spoke forcefully.

'I'm Josephine Moran, Mr Mason, I'm in poster drafting... my husband would be horrified if he found out I was working to support the BNU. We are a Christian couple and we see the BNU as an evil on Earth, an ally and promoter of all that is wrong in our society. I am sure there are others here who for different reasons find the BNU and its neo-Nazi policies abhorrent. You cannot justify getting this agency to support the BNU... many of us will not.'

He allowed the short diatribe to settle as he digested her comments, as he did so he heard voices approving her stance.

'Mrs Moran... Josephine if I may... I am fully aware of what the BNU stands for and I want it known that the decision to agree their promotion was not lightly made – it was an agonizingly difficult decision. However, given the size of the contract, and the fact that I am duty-bound to protect your livelihoods and the survival of this agency – a decision against signing the agreement was out of the question. Now, to set your minds at rest, one of the conditions of the contract is that the BNU will moderate their policies and in no way promote extreme and unpalatable attitudes. Their political officers will work alongside us; anything we think is distasteful cannot, under the contractual terms and conditions, be included in the promotion. Furthermore, as an incentive, for the duration of the campaign, staff will get an additional one month's salary every month. At the end of our involvement with the BNU work, everyone on staff will get a two thousand pound bonus tax-free. Senior staff members and team leaders will receive a proportionately higher bonus. Those of you who are still bewildered as to why we contracted with the BNU may now get the idea that it was entirely for the sake of the agency and its staff. You will be well rewarded for your efforts and it is highly doubtful you will be outraged by any part of the promotion – after all, you will be the moderators.'

As he finished there was what appeared to be a resentful hush among the staff; for a moment or two no one moved or said anything. Then Sam Taylor came forward and stood at the front.

'I know how many of you feel and I can't say I am particularly comfortable with the situation. However, it would be wrong to condemn Elliot for taking the decision that has been made. Apart from the recent Autoclean project, as an agency we have been on notice that if we did not improve turnover and profit margins we were facing a very uncertain future. This BNU contract is, to say the least, extremely lucrative. Not only directly for staff, as Elliot says during the life of the contract, but for a long way into the future. In short, everyone, Elliot has thrown us a lifeline. We would be stupid to reject it purely on moral grounds – I don't think our families would take a moral point of view if the mortgage wasn't paid, they had no heating, were about to be evicted onto the streets and hadn't eaten for a few days. Come on! Let's be pragmatic about this, after all – we can control the campaign. Let's not cut off our nose to spite our face.'

Sam finished with a smile, facing the crowd and willing them to see sense.

For a few seconds there were only a few shuffled feet and pensive attitudes. Then a few voices said 'OK', a few others 'you know we do need it' and yet others simply nodded their heads. Seconds followed and then they were all discussing it among themselves.

Now Mason had to follow up on Sam Taylor's comments

to reinforce the wave of agreement – even a few dissenting heads might yet damage his plans.

Lifting his voice above the ever-rising clamour, he gave one last reassurance to convince the doubters.

'We may not like it but we will rise above it, of that I am sure. Remember please, we are a democracy – regardless of ideology, democracies win. Look at the overriding success of pre-unification West Germany compared to the East, of how economic success came to Singapore and Japan after becoming democratic. What about South Korea compared to its impoverished northern neighbour? Yes, it is a flawed system, but at least everyone has their say and it underscores freedom and human rights. We may have doubts about working for the BNU but if we don't, someone else will. What we can do is curb any extreme content in the broadcasts, and by God we will. Thank you everyone – let's get on.'

As they filed out of the cafeteria Mason felt a wave of relief; with luck all would progress normally, it was just a matter of getting the final broadcasts modulated. It mattered not what had been approved or disputed by his staff or the BNU – the BNU would get what they wanted.

As he sat in reflection on the morning's staff encounter the intercom buzzer called for attention. He flipped the intercom receive switch and heard Margaret's soft voice. 'Nigel Armstrong has arrived but as yet there is no sign of Simon Rogers. Shall I send Nigel in?'

Why not? Simon would turn up eventually.

'Yes please Margaret and would you arrange coffee for three please – no, make that four, you deserve one too.'

He heard a slight exhalation of appreciation and then the intercom went dead. Moments later his office door opened and a smiling Nigel Armstrong walked in.

'Good morning Elliot, trust you are well?'

He was indeed; as things stood, in a few short days he was on course to walk away with £10 million.

'Nigel, good to see you. What happened to Simon?'

Armstrong took a front seat and raised his hands in frustration and ignorance.

'I left a message that I would meet him at the station rather than round him up and drag him away from his VDUs. When he didn't turn up I assumed he had gone on ahead since there was no answer from his phone. If he's true to form he'll be getting here by Intercity and Tube – via Leeds I should think, if they don't put him off at Glasgow! We should give him another ten minutes to find his way here. That said I have some interesting data you should know about.'

Mason sat down, looking forward to what Armstrong had to say.

'I'm all ears.'

'That small scrap of paper you let me have – in Emma Lilton's handwriting – regarding deconditioning. I pondered on it for a while and a few things occurred to me. The first was that a few years back one of my students ran an experiment that amassed a large set of electro encephalograms – the brain activities of a lot of ordinary people. By chance, a current student had reason to do the same, and he too obtained a decent set of brainwaves from several hundred subjects recently exposed to TV. Now, if delta modulation had a profound effect on people's brainwave patterns it would show up by comparing one set against another – the old data would be normal, the new data should show a larger range of discrepancies or abnormalities. What I found is interesting; the recent set displayed a small number of delta wave abnormalities, similar to those from subjects with obsessive-compulsive disorder. If I am right—'

A staccato knocking came from the office door and Simon Rogers slipped in to the office. With enormous care he silently closed the door behind him and crept up to a chair next to Armstrong.

He waited until Rogers had seated himself, somewhat amused by the way Nigel Armstrong looked to the heavens as Simon settled.

'Good to see you, Simon. Got delayed, did you?' He half winked in Nigel Armstrong's direction, a gesture that Simon Rogers entirely failed to notice.

'Er... Yes. Got too immersed in my work, lost track of time. Very close to getting to where I want to go, so I didn't like to stop.'

'Glad to hear it, Simon. Nigel was telling me about a comparison of brainwave patterns between different subjects, those exposed to recent TV broadcasts and those a few years ago, wherein we assume the recent lot got sight of the Autoclean commercial. Some had different delta wave patterns to those from a long-past survey. You were saying, Nigel?'

'Oh yes, some had delta wave abnormalities akin to people with obsessive-compulsive disorders. My guess is that the delta wave modulation simulates or imitates the patterns akin to such a disorder resulting in similar behaviour. What is even more interesting is that I took a small batch of EEGs from some students who admitted watching the Autoclean commercials, but only a very small number showed residual delta wave disruption. Though not conclusive by a long way it does indicate that the effect, if there is one, tends to wear off. In short, it isn't a permanent effect; it recedes with time. In some it recedes quicker than in others, because it depends on the depth of the imprinting and the subject's particular psychology. However, in time I suspect all those exposed to delta imprinting will naturally decondition.'

It gave him food for thought.

'OK Nigel, if you are right then that is very reassuring. We can assume that the modulation does not create long-term damage. Now, *à propos* that, I want you to listen very closely to what I have to say. This agency has just signed an agreement with the British National Union to compose and promote their upcoming general election campaign. I'm fully aware...'

Nigel Armstrong nearly choked as he heard what was being said and suddenly stood up.

'Jesus Christ, Elliot – do you know what you are saying? The BNU are a Neo-Nazi party, they advocate a totalitarian regime, as bad as Germany in the 1930s and after. Their leadership wants to do everything the Nazis did – it would be a national disaster if they obtained any parliamentary influence.'

Mason waited as Armstrong finished his furious denunciation, giving an outraged and haunted look. He held back replying, turning his attention momentarily to Simon Rogers who remained seated but looking somewhat bewildered. However, Rogers wasn't protesting.

'Hold your horses, Nigel, and please hear me out. The BNU electoral campaign will be conventional – we will monitor the content, nothing extreme will be included. Furthermore, I am able to offer each of you one million pounds for your confidentiality and your willingness to delta modulate the electoral party political broadcasts. With that kind of money, paid in cash immediately, I get back the modulated video copies and you are free to enjoy yourselves. The only other condition is that you teach Sam Taylor, the agency's head of CGI, how to delta modulate our videos. This is not intended to displace you two but in case you are... let's say... indisposed at any time, I can fall back on Sam. Think hard... with that kind of money your options are universal;

you could escape all your commitments and concerns. Come on, it's more than enough to sway your principles and leave you independent.'

Nigel Armstrong retook his seat looking preoccupied. There was now a tense atmosphere that left him unsure of the outcome. Then he saw Armstrong's head come up and lock eyes with him.

'One million you say – on completion?'

'Yeah, and in case you haven't considered it, think on this. My guess is that no matter how moderate or persuasive our TV campaign is, few will actually bother to watch it. I suspect that most of the population will refuse to watch a BNU broadcast on principle. As such, regardless of the delta modulation, the number of converts will turn out to be minimal.'

As before, neither Nigel Armstrong nor Rogers made comment, instead it was clear each had good reason to stay silent. Armstrong needed time to battle with his conscience; Rogers was indifferent because he had too little experience to give him a perspective on the enormity and consequences of the project.

At last, after an almost interminable period of time had passed, Nigel Armstrong simply said 'OK, Elliot, but I do it under protest and for one million pounds. Money first.'

He smiled, noting that Simon Rogers, once again, took the position of a spectator.

'Goodness, Nigel, don't you trust me? You will have to wait I'm afraid until the political broadcasts are finalized and I can give you the videos. It means that I can't pay you until all of it is complete – six to seven months time I'm sorry to tell you. However, you are each due a bonus for your efforts so far, I'll get finance to advance you another thousand each. How's that?'

The two in front of him looked at each other and with an almost imperceptible nod of heads gave a silent agreement.

'OK – where do we find this Sam Taylor you spoke of? We need to liaise with him,' Armstrong said.

'I'll arrange for him to come and see you over the next few months, there's no rush.'

Mason realized that Rogers had played no part in the recent exchange with Armstrong and he needed to be certain that Rogers was still bound to the project.

'Simon – are you comfortable with all this – do you agree with the deal?'

Surprised at being put on the spot, Rogers gave a slight jump in his chair and shook his head.

'No! What's your objection?'

'Uh, none really – sounds very generous to me. It's just that I've no political leanings; I know nothing about this British National Union. I'll go with Nigel on this. Anyway, I'm close to writing up my PhD thesis. I'll need six months to get on with it and what needs to be done to the videos won't take more than half an hour – so, whenever it's time, it's OK with me.'

He smiled back at Rogers; he was in the bag.

It was time to close the meeting. He had succeeded – but only just! Now he had to mend the slight gulf that had arisen between him and Nigel Armstrong.

'Don't brood over this, Nigel, it's simply a means to an end. Just think, with all that money, you can make all your academic colleagues wish they were you.'

Armstrong gave a hint of a smile. 'On that subject, we'll stop by in finance on the way out – trust you'll get to them before we do.'

He nodded approval and stood ready to shake hands with Armstrong and Rogers.

'Doing anything nice this evening, you two? Got a girl-friend, Simon?'

Rogers gave a shy smile and shook his head. As he turned to Nigel Armstrong and took his hand he saw he had now relented his antipathy and was presenting a slight grin.

'I'm on a date tonight – a lovely girl.'

'Really? Good for you. You must introduce me some time.'

As Armstrong turned away he said, 'No need, you know her already, I'm taking Margaret out... your secretary.'

For a second the remark didn't penetrate, and then he felt the blow.

He'd been too preoccupied to follow through on his intention to court Margaret. Now it seemed he was too late. If he was to catch up he would have to tread strategically and carefully – he wanted to keep his money, and he wanted Margaret too.

Chapter 16

THE OPENING FEW weeks with the BNU representatives in the agency had been tense, if not heavy with animosity. It had to be said that the BNU people took it in their stride, and to all appearances refused to be deterred by their reception.

It was clear that they had been briefed to ride the difficulties they were likely to confront, and to use politeness and charm to allay the feelings of agency staff. Slowly the atmosphere softened and occasionally a burst of laughter would indicate a thawing of the usual icy climate. It took all of six weeks in some cases but as the scripts for the broadcasts and the eventual interviews with BNU leaders started to accumulate and be recorded and edited, it became a routine process.

Mason began to watch the 'rushes' of the interviews, short commercials and the mock-ups for the poster campaigns with a sense of relief and surprise. As far as he could judge, the content was neutral in terms of the BNU's avowed policies. The BNU party line was hard to distinguish amongst the highlighting of the current administration's cock-ups and failures. Most of the subject matter focused on what the current administration had promised in their manifesto, and had then conveniently ignored when in government. False promises had thrived, so too their handling of ministerial scandals. Likewise, criticism was aimed at the main opposition parties, for their weakness and hypocrisy when it came to unpopular legislation instigated by the ruling party. In short, the whole of the scripting, editing and visual insertions in the programmes made for a hard-hitting campaign that made it clear that no one in their right mind would, or should, vote for any other party except the BNU.

As he and a gaggle of BNU party officials viewed each of the four separate BNU party political broadcasts that were to be televised, he sat with Michael Benson and Nicholas Frobisher, one row behind the BNU's party leader, Alex Feldt, himself flanked by his number two, one Neil Middleton. As each appearance of Feldt and Middleton took place on screen, the small audience gave a round of applause. It occurred to him that the agency scriptwriters and editorial staff had excelled – Feldt made an almost charismatic appearance in every showing, leaving no one in any doubt about the old adage 'sincerity is the thing, if you can fake it you've got it made'.

As each of the broadcasts were screened, Mason received complimentary comments from everyone around him. His gratification was heightened by the remarks from the front row that the decision to retain Morley, Swan & Bramly for the BNU's campaign had been the right one. The final reassurance came from Nicholas Frobisher who, leaning over to him between viewings, confirmed that the final payment of £27 million had been authorized. When Benson asked if they were watching clean or 'tweaked' versions of the broadcasts, he told him that changes had yet to be made, but the modified ones, those to be transmitted, would go out to the TV channels in a month's time. Benson only commented that he trusted Elliot would keep his word and nothing less.

The implied threat was unnecessary – he knew what he had to do.

As more and more flattering observations came his way he realized that for all the risks he had taken, his money was safe, the agency was safe, and all was right with the world. There was now only the one other thing that needed doing, and for that he had to rely on Simon Rogers, Nigel Armstrong and Sam Taylor.

Sam Taylor sat in front of him, apparently relaxed and attentive.

Taylor had finished with the limited CGI involvement required by the BNU work and was busy with a conventional toothpaste advertisement that had been commissioned halfway through all the political work.

'I take it you've covered everything that Simon Rogers and Nigel Armstrong discovered about the Autoclean commercial. I assume that if push came to shove you could replicate the delta wave modulation in the same way they would. Can I rely on that?'

Taylor gave a slow shake of his head implying indecision.

'In simple terms yes, by simply copying a previous modulation, say from a previous copy of the Autoclean video. What I don't know, because it's beyond my expertise, is how to determine what level of modulation does what – they've yet to discuss this aspect with me. Furthermore, Nigel was talking about reducing the delta wave modulation to a lower frequency, that is two cycles per second. He says it is probably far more generic and likely to be more effective. Ask me to do what the Autoclean ad did and I think I could do it, but at the moment no more than that.'

He considered the consequence of Taylor's remarks and dismissed the negative aspects of it. After all, should he ever be solely reliant on Sam Taylor, it would mean that he no longer had access to Armstrong or Rogers, and that seemed a most remote possibility.

'OK Sam, do what you need to do to learn more from our friends – I expect that eventually you will gather more about the delta stuff as you engage with the two of them. In the meantime, I'm awarding you a twenty thousand pound bonus over and above what the other staff will get, and I also want you to sign a non-disclosure agreement. The NDA is to put you on the same footing as Armstrong and Rogers – they've both signed one. The award is for your past adherence and loyalty in keeping silent about the mystery behind the Autoclean commercial – I know you had your suspicions from the start. It's also to thank you for your help during the BNU address I gave to the staff; it's much appreciated. You will be one of a very small circle of people that know about our subliminal imprinting. I would like it to stay that way. Are you agreeable?'

Taylor nodded, a look of pleasure crossing his face.

'No problem Elliot, I'll be happy to comply, as I have already.'

'Good – how goes the other work, any way forward on the Delicream assignment?'

Taylor gave a further nod. 'Almost complete, I'll get the edited version to you by tomorrow.'

'Good, I look forward to seeing it. Incidentally, I assume everyone else has taken the news about their payments and bonuses with pleasure. No regrets about working with the BNU?'

'As far as I can see, none – we have a very happy team at the moment.'

He felt a ripple of pleasure himself. It had all come to a very satisfactory conclusion.

Chapter 17

O<small>N THE DAY</small> Nigel Armstrong came to his office to deliver the modulated versions of the forthcoming BNU broadcasts, Mason had a sneaky feeling that as Armstrong passed through Margaret's office it had been a rapid and unexpectedly brief excursion.

Over the last few months he had seen Margaret change. Her silent mourning for Jonathan Woodbridge had receded; she had emerged as a more outgoing and talkative individual. Her adherence to being a highly professional and perfectly attired secretary had not diminished one iota, but her return to a vibrant and sociable behaviour indicated that she had shed much of her grief and was now far less crushed by the loss of her fiancé. He assumed that this was Nigel Armstrong's doing. However, the last week or two had seen yet another change in her, and he suspected that all was not right between the two of them.

He had reluctantly refrained from trying to impose himself on Margaret while she and Nigel Armstrong were dating. Competing with Armstrong could have created all kinds of unnecessary problems – he didn't want to have to contend with a jealous suitor, too many vital targets would have been at risk.

However, if his suspicions were correct, Margaret and

Nigel Armstrong were not as close now as they were. Perhaps Margaret was available again. He would see.

From Nigel Armstrong's demeanour it didn't appear as though he was hurt or troubled by anything. He sat, apparently relaxed, in the centre seat in front of the desk and responded in a neutral and controlled way.

As he took hold of the stack of DVDs and video cassettes Armstrong had delivered, he acknowledged their receipt gratefully.

'All done then Nigel, I assume you and Simon didn't need to spend too long on these.'

Armstrong shook his head and pointed at the stack.

'Our only problem was the level of delta modulation to be used. We didn't know for sure how many times these broadcasts were likely to be screened, so we had to assume a minimum number of viewings rather than a repeated transmission like a commercial. To cater for a lower number of broadcasts we upped the modulation to eighteen per cent and reduced the delta frequency to two cycles per second. This latter because it meets the modern criteria for a generic delta wave – we think it is likely to be more effective. Since we watched the unmodulated videos as a matter of course, we have to say we were very impressed. As stand-alone productions they are very persuasive – please pass on our congratulations to the production team, even a political novice like Simon thought they were all very shrewd and hard hitting.'

It was gratifying to hear Armstrong's comments, on more than one front. It confirmed his own opinion of his team's excellent work; not only that but the high quality of the productions reduced the chances of anyone asking awkward questions about the impact of the broadcasts.

'Glad to hear that, Nigel. Of course, I don't have to tell you not to watch the TV versions, do I?'

'I won't be watching anything – I won't be here for the election period, I'm off on a long sabbatical. Won't even get a chance to vote – not that it would have any significance even if I did.'

Armstrong's unexpected announcement was a surprise.

'Where are you planning to go, and what about Simon? I thought you were his PhD supervisor.'

Armstrong drooped his head as though burdened and weary.

'I'm going to lose myself for a while, get over a few disappointments and maybe begin the book I've always promised myself I would write. I'm tempted to resign from the university – as I said, I have other plans. As for Simon, I'm not his supervisor, Jeffrey Innes is, and Simon's still writing up his thesis. As soon as it's done and approved Jeffrey will arrange Simon's viva voce at short notice. It's not a problem. Simon tells me he's completing his writing up at home – at his parents' house – and will be incommunicado for a while. It means we'll both be absent for some deserved leave for a few months. In any case, except for a dire emergency you won't need Simon or me – well, not in the short term anyway. You will have to depend on Sam Taylor as a fire brigade. If you do have an urgent need to find us, here's Simon's contact address and telephone number. He, in turn, will know where to find me. OK?'

Mason gave a nod of his head in acknowledgement – he was in no position to object to either Armstrong's or Rogers' decision to disappear for a time. On the face of it, it was somewhat disappointing, but what Armstrong had noted was for the moment true – unless he was planning to do anything crucial Armstrong and Rogers weren't that necessary. Were he to decide that in the interim he would modulate a conventional commercial then Sam Taylor was the fall-back expert – certainly in terms of matching the

Autoclean campaign.

'Well Nigel, OK. I do hope I see you again, refreshed and re-invigorated I'm sure. I've no idea where you intend to go but no doubt you can now afford it. As a matter of interest, what has Simon decided to do with his... windfall?'

Armstrong gave a hint of a smile. 'I'm not absolutely sure Elliot, he hardly made mention of it after we received the money. It could be he's bought a satellite navigation system to ensure he finds his way around. Other than that, I can't think of what he would spend his money on. As for me, it's blue skies and golden sands in southern Portugal for a short while and then... a refuge somewhere; one with a keyboard, a kettle and lots of coffee.'

His heart leapt. Armstrong had made no mention of Margaret in his plans, so perhaps his suspicions were right.

'Well, good for you Nigel, I wish you *bon voyage*. If you make a definite decision to resign your present profession let me know – especially if you are interested in further developments on the subliminal side and want something to do.'

He shook hands with a vacant-faced and seemingly morose Armstrong, and watched as he turned quickly and made his way out. He hoped for some conversation to creep in through the open door as Armstrong entered Margaret's office, but all he heard were soft footsteps and silence.

As he regained his chair it occurred to him that like Nigel Armstrong, he could now dispense with the constant urge to advance his career and income. Now he had all the resources he needed not to continue as he was. There was nothing stopping him from resigning his post and falling back on his recently well-stocked bank account. With care and good investment he need never work again. And yet, he was proud and protective of his hard-won position as agency chief. It was the combination of status and pride that he valued, and he was deeply reluctant to squander all it entailed. No! He wasn't overly inclined to throw it all away – he liked things as they were.

But a break, a short vacation for rest and recreation somewhere, with Margaret for company, might refresh everything and give him a chance to make Margaret appreciate him a little more. He could leave Sam Taylor in charge for a while. The teams had their own momentum and his diary told him he had no imminent negotiations for project sign-offs or forthcoming meetings with clients; it meant he wouldn't be missed for a week or ten days. His board of directors would be unlikely to grumble, he had already received a letter of thanks from the chairman noting the major improvements in the profit and loss ledger and indicating that his position would definitely be ratified at the next board meeting.

He pressed the intercom toggle switch.

Margaret didn't respond immediately but then a slightly husky voice came from the speaker.

'Yes Elliot?'

'Margaret, I'm awarding you a bonus – it's a surprise – finance will notify you how much it is. Furthermore I would like you to book two first-class seats for Barbados and book into a top-notch hotel. Make reservations for two. Book everything for a ten-day stay.'

Again, for a moment there was hesitation in her reply.

'For two you say, Elliot... confirm?'

'Yes, you and me Margaret, and please don't argue. You deserve a break as I do. I'm taking you away as an enormous thank you for all you have done for me during my time here. Because of that, I promise you the time of your life.'

All he heard was a slight sob and, 'Oh thank you Elliot!'

Chapter 18

THE BLUE SKY and warm white sands of the beach joined with the lapping turquoise sea, forming a hazy horizon as he lay with his back on a beach towel in the hot sunshine. Margaret Delaney lay to his right, sunning herself on an airbed and clad in a bikini that revealed her exquisite figure. He had enjoyed her company for a week now and after he had broken the ice by arranging a candlelit dinner on their first night in the hotel, he discovered that the initial physical attraction he felt for her had been supplemented by a wonderfully erudite and elated personality. She was a joy, and he wondered how she managed to constantly portray the formal, fastidious and thoroughly professional secretary that she was. Now, as he thought about the trip back to the UK, he asked himself whether he wanted to let go of this idyllic episode in his life. If truth be told there was no earthly reason why he should go back home; it was just a matter of letting go of his ambitions for a while and renouncing his claims to the status he'd built up. It was very tempting to see what might transpire were he to plump for a domestic existence with Margaret – should she agree to have him – and settle for the gentle life of a man of independent means. Would he cope having his days occupied by golf, fishing and social gatherings?

Perhaps not!

The thought stirred a sense of loss in his mind and once again he reluctantly allowed himself to listen to the nagging voice that kept reminding him of his history and what he had become. Just before they had made the trip here, he had battled with his conscience about giving up the race. And, as before, he knew he could not abandon all that he had fought for.

What was it he had concluded?

That it was the combination of status and pride that he valued, and he was unwilling to squander all it entailed.

With a slight sigh of acquiescence he turned onto his stomach, feeling the sun's heat flood over his back and legs and, by turning his head, seeing Margaret's sleeping curves. He noticed her left hand, now devoid of Jonathan Woodbridge's engagement ring even though she had retained his eternity ring. Nigel Armstrong had not managed to gain her love, but with luck he, Elliot Mason, would succeed. However, he was at risk of losing her if going back meant he wasn't able to give her the time and affection she deserved. He was going to have to ensure he didn't neglect her, and yet be able to do his job as it should be done. He had to win Margaret and yet retain his sense of worth. It was going to be tricky but he couldn't see why it should fail.

On the flight back Margaret slept peacefully with her head slumped against his shoulder. They had plumped for seats in business class because their aircraft had been over-booked on first class. It meant an overnight stay near the airport if they were to get the first-class seats they had paid for on the next departing flight. They were so engaged with one another that the disappointment hardly registered, and still wrapped around each other they had taken a conciliatory attitude to the airline staff and smiled openly as their less luxurious seats were arranged. The refund offered was barely acknowledged – he didn't need it, not with his new wife-to-be on his arm. He couldn't stop smiling – life was good!

As Margaret slumbered he was able to read some of the day-old UK newspapers that had been handed out by the cabin stewards. With Margaret's body nestled into his, he had only the one arm completely free so it was a difficult exercise opening the pages of the newspapers. Nevertheless, he was able to survey most of the front pages of the tabloids, the majority of which carried pre-election news. There appeared to be a general consensus that the current Tory government would once again carry the country. However, some of the leading articles noted, in closing, that this would be the first election where nearly every seat would be contested by a British National Union candidate. Some even wondered how it was that the BNU had the organization and funds to field so many candidates. It was the general belief that most would lose their deposit.

As he read the clearly dismissive comments in the press he allowed himself a wry smile. If the BNU party political broadcasts he had overseen had the effect he expected, the political commentators in the press were going to have to eat their hats. And yet, as the thought came to him, he felt a slight involuntary shudder. Was he prepared for the consequences of an extreme right-wing party gaining power? Would he regret his decision to get into bed with Benson, Frobisher, Middleton and Feldt? What kind of world would they impose on the country – was it for good or for bad? But then, now it was too late for regrets; after all, he had stayed loyal to his priorities, even though they were at one and the same time selfish and yet altruistic.

All he could do was to wait and see – his hesitant marriage

proposal to Margaret had not been rejected, to his joy she had smiled and said yes, on condition that he booked the honeymoon at the same resort. So, regardless of national politics his marriage came first and, for the time being, everything else was secondary.

When they returned to the agency together on the next Monday morning, most of the staff were waiting to receive them. The applause was both gratifying and a little embarrassing, especially when Sam Taylor came forward and congratulated them on their engagement. It came as a shock: he had no idea how the news had preceded them, and it was only later in his office that Margaret confessed that she had contacted Sam to ensure nothing had happened during their absence that might mar their homecoming. It was clear that no matter her newfound status, she had lost none of her proficiency as a top-line secretary.

As the day wore on he was pleased to discover that all current projects in the agency were on target. Sam Taylor reported that the Delicream commercial was ready for viewing and approval, the posters for the London Underground were complete and three other projects requiring both voiceovers and archive insertions were moving forward very well. As for the new Autoclean commercial, that too was nearing finalization. It was up to him to decide if the same 'process' was to be applied. Sam simply left the idea hanging.

He found himself well pleased with progress and began to look at his forthcoming meetings with various corporate worthies. It was clear that the agency had attracted a lot of interest from advertisers. He expected that his job would be easier from now on – he had no need to hard sell what they could do. The 'word' had definitely got around.

As he was completing some administrative paperwork,

Margaret came in.

'Elliot, the first BNU party political broadcast is going out tonight on all channels. What do you want to do?'

He gave it a brief thought.

'It's something we should definitely ignore. Let's go out to dinner – what do you think?'

'Sounds like an excellent idea – we think alike,' she said.

It was later that evening, sitting at a candlelit table in a nearby bistro, that he took Margaret's left hand and held it tight, as though in need of closeness and comfort. She noted that his mood had begun to change. His attention to her and their surroundings would intermittently wander, and she would watch him slip into a self-absorbed and introspective state. Margaret was quick to sense his concern, and asked him about it in a sympathetic tone.

'Penny for them – are you still with me?'

He found it hard to tell her that, though there was nothing directly ominous he could identify, he harboured a sense of foreboding that had worsened on their return to the agency. Why he felt it, and why he was preoccupied by it, he found hard to explain. Yet he could not shake off a feeling of impending trouble. It had arisen following Margaret's acceptance of his marriage proposal. Like all couples, he looked forward to a long, happy and successful marriage, but somehow the imminent screening of the BNU party political broadcasts cast a shadow over that expectation. The fact that he now saw his natural responsibility to his fiancée in far more focused terms was one thing, but the underlying reason for this over-protective attitude was somehow BNU-oriented. It was logically inconsistent that he should be alarmed by something he had directed and overseen and that offered no clear or direct threat to his future. But it was akin to being the designer of an atomic bomb – if it actually succeeded in detonating, there was no going back.

He put his left hand over the top of his right, which was now holding Margaret's left, and clasped them together. He looked at her with an earnest expression.

'Sorry if I appear preoccupied, Margaret. I can't tell you how happy you have made me. I'm deeply flattered in every respect that we are to be married. I love you and I want us to look forward to a long life together, but I have a few reasons to be apprehensive about the forthcoming election. All I'm going to say about it is this: if the day comes when we cannot be sure about our security, I want you to go and stay with your mother. I'm not being paranoid, I'm thinking of you and what I see as a contingency plan. If you trust me, remember what I have just said.'

She gave a slight stiffening of her shoulders and looked into his eyes intently. For a long time, she said nothing, then a slight smile crossed her lips.

'Paranoid you would never be, Elliot Mason. Yes, I hear what you say. Let's hope your contingency plan is just a pointless proposal. I certainly hope so.'

Chapter 19

THE CHANGE IN public comment and the TV news reports, as too articles in various newspapers regarding the BNU campaign, was subtle but nonetheless noticeable. As the first two BNU political broadcasts received their TV transmissions, complimentary if not flattering comments slowly superseded the derogatory, disparaging and occasional insulting comments usually reserved for the BNU. Feldt, the BNU's leader, was granted a high approval rating by most of the pre-election pollsters for his insightful and pragmatic comments when on screen. Even when he announced that the party would increase income and corporation tax by 1 per cent to pay for improved health services and to augment the armed services, there were no media protests. It was also noted that the extreme policies of the BNU, expected to be disclosed during the broadcasts, were either muted or left unspoken throughout the presentations; indeed, one commentator noted that had he not known better, it was not the BNU he knew that was being given TV airtime, rather, some middle-of-the-road party. There was, he noted, not a hint of any remote or extreme ideology. He could have been forgiven, he said, for thinking he was watching a party political broadcast on behalf of the Christian Democrat Party.

He watched with incredulous interest as the polls began to indicate a definite shift in public opinion and much of the people's intention to vote. Each succeeding broadcast by the BNU reinforced their growing popularity and, he had to admit it, he was beginning to be unsure whether the subliminal effect explained the change or because the broadcasts were so well structured and directed. Indeed, he began to feel quite proud of his team's expertise and professionalism. It was hard to fault the level of persuasion in all the scripts composed for the featured party members, or to criticize the general appeal to the average voter's opinion about how government should act. There was no doubt about it; it was becoming one hell of a campaign.

Two days before polling day he decided to arrange another break for Margaret and himself. He wanted to be in a different environment when the results of the election came in. He knew that most of the agency teams would be watching some, or all, of the political broadcasts. He had no intention of being in close proximity to over-enthusiastic members of staff – either because of the gratification they obtained by seeing their work on TV or because of the way the election had gone. Both might well arise in any one individual. Besides himself and Margaret, the only other agency member who would know why the election might swing towards the BNU was Sam Taylor. What Sam was going to do was for him to decide; he and Margaret would be just as far from the electoral celebrations as possible, and away from any comeback if the BNU campaign failed.

Chapter 20

THINKING BACK TO the night the election results were announced, he and Margaret had managed to avoid any awareness of how well the various parties were doing. They had rented a cottage near Bangor in north Wales and had spent a great deal of time exploring the area around the Menai Straits and into Anglesey itself, finding it fairly easy to avoid any contact with the media outlets. But it was inevitable that they would at last come to know what had happened and when on the second day after the election Margaret brought back a tabloid newspaper, its headline 'BNU Take Power With Landslide' told the whole story.

According to reports, it was an overwhelming victory for the BNU, with hardly any other party making headway. It was unprecedented; the other parties – even the long established and usually popular ones – had been ousted by the BNU in almost every constituency. So much so, that as things stood Parliament would see a BNU majority so substantial that they would have no problem passing legislation – their majority exceeded 200.

When Alex Feldt, now the new prime minister, came on TV to announce his party's daunting task in forming a new government, he spoke of 'the grave responsibility of changing the face of Britain' and his gratitude to the British people for 'creating a sea change in British politics' to the point where it constituted a 'revolution'. He spoke of a 'serious democratic discrepancy' in modern politics and quoted Shakespeare in lambasting previous administrations for their 'insolence of office'. The nation would benefit from a 'new and strong government not afraid to tackle difficult issues'.

His relaxed and soft intonation while speaking gave no reason to think that the revolution he spoke of would be anything more than a little tinkering with the way things were; that it would all be the same, but different.

Now, as he thought back to those innocent days, he – and many millions of others – could not have foreseen what the term 'revolution' really meant.

Had they been able to do so, the grim, derelict and forbidding country they now occupied would not have come about.

As his thoughts meandered through all the disruption and desecration the new government had created in the culture and disposition of the British population, he began to increasingly regret his decision to use the subliminal imprinting to enhance the BNU's party political broadcasts. The irony was that two days after the election Nicholas Frobisher, soon to be the new minister of finance (the title of chancellor was abolished) phoned to congratulate him on the fine work carried out in producing the BNU's party political broadcast. He had even hinted that there might be an 'honour' forthcoming and promised that Morley, Swan & Bramly would always be the agency of choice for the BNU.

As he now saw it, what had transpired following the BNU victory wasn't worth a hundred times what he had accepted.

At first, he recalled, life had followed the usual mundane routine with very little to indicate that a radical government was now in power. It was clear that the minor parliamentary presence of the few non-BNU seats made no difference to the BNU plans. The voices of the opposition were not just muted but also effectively silenced.

The agency's normality seemed oddly intimidating as, on the face of it at least, they handled the same kind of commissions and competed against the same range of problems, while all the time watching restrictive irritations come to the fore as the new administration began its 'revolution'.

It was as he sat idly scanning the progress reports of two current commercials in development that Margaret came into his office carrying a large manila envelope.

'Hello darling – what's this?'

'It's just arrived, Elliot – delivered by hand. It's an official D notice… a ban on the appearance or publication of certain subjects.'

'The what?'

He looked at the three sheets marked as emanating from the new Ministry of Home Security. They were all entitled 'Ethnic and Social Diversity – Restrictions on Approving, Featuring or Inclusion of Non-Caucasian Ethnic Categories Or Non-Christian Religions in Media and Advertising.'

He read the title and gasped.

Margaret came around to his side of the desk as he read further, absorbing the details of what was now illegal according to the MHS.

He shook his head. 'They've banned all appearances in advertising of ethnic types… only whites from now on… and nothing that gives exposure or prominence either to non-Christian religions or to other cultures. We can't even mention them, let alone feature anything visual to do with them. Not only that, articles or features that exalt or praise non-white ethnic groups is forbidden. No TV programmes can show non-white actors. The appearance of a black male with a white woman partner in TV programmes or commercials is absolutely proscribed, with severe penalties in default. In short, cultural diversity is dead. It seems the BNU has come out of its shell; all the BNU policies everyone so loathed in the past are coming home to roost.'

'What do we do Elliot? Two of our current projects have non-whites featured in them.'

'Comply I suppose. We have little choice. Can you get the two project leaders in here in the next half hour – they will have to start again I'm afraid. Oh, and contact Steve Mitchell at the Mail, see if the newspapers and the TV stations have had the same D notice too. Christ, I wish...'

'What Elliot, you wish what?'

He gave a despondent look. 'Nothing darling, other than the fact that I am beginning to feel that you and I have done our bit for the advertising sector and it's time to go.'

Margaret put her arms around him. 'Don't be defeatist – this is a minor setback. Everything will be all right.'

He turned, reached up, and kissed her. 'Hope you're right – I really do.'

Were he able to turn the clock back, he would have been tempted to tell Benson and Frobisher what to do with the BNU commission and would certainly have refused the huge bribe he had taken. It was time for regrets.

The two poster artists and the team leader vacated his office in a dejected mood. Their project was almost finalized and now it meant a new start with the completion deadline only three weeks away. He'd suggested that the inclusion of a black man in the setting could be revamped so that the amendments would only require making the figure white instead of black. This suggestion was received with woeful looks – it was easier, they said, to start from scratch.

He let them go with expressions of regret – the news about the D notice would spread and he hoped that no one else was working on anything that would contravene the restrictions.

He decided to show himself around the work areas and offer staff the opportunity to speak to him. It was intended to placate the more principled of his staff and explain the situation to all the others.

He passed the canteen on his way onto the main floor and heard raised voices coming through the entrance. As he stopped, and looked in, the canteen was empty except for two of the CGI staff sitting at a table. It was obvious that they were having a heated debate, but all he heard was the tail end.

'... Bastards... think of all the work we've done on the Fisbury animation – now it's gone to pot. And to think, I voted for the shits. Even now, I can't for the life of me work out why I bothered. Christ, I'd love to get my hands on...'

'For God's sake will you calm down – we can remedy the animation, its only three scenes. If you continue speaking your mind you are likely to run into trouble. If its any consolation, I voted the same way as you did; were you to ask me why I voted BNU I couldn't tell you. But it's too late now, we have to grin and bear it... more's the pity.'

He continued on to the work floor feeling increasingly guilty and taking the view that if the rest of the population were becoming as discontent as some members of his staff, it did not bode well.

Nevertheless, as he approached various working groups he was heartened by the approving reception he received. They hadn't forgotten his generosity during the BNU project. Only occasionally did he hear a complaint or a gripe and even then it was muted and far from personal.

He returned to his office somewhat more encouraged by his staff, though still pessimistic as far as the general future of the country was concerned.

Chapter 21

THE ORDER TO make sedition and disaffection a criminal offence appeared in the media a month later. The new administration was determined to consolidate and, where necessary, increase their power and influence. As regards the new order on sedition, they had considered the matter a priority to avoid 'subversive voices damaging the economy and the cohesiveness of the state'.

It applied to the newspapers and any other form of publication irrespective of the D notices already in force. There was no appeal to law, the Supreme Court was forthwith abolished and lawyers were barred from defending 'anyone charged with offences against the state'.

To Elliot Mason the ever-increasing protests, both private and occasionally public, were indicative of a growing awareness that they were facing a cynical and insidious totalitarian authority in their new government. What was also obvious was the fact that the BNU had no intention of letting go of their ideology or the right-wing policies they had failed to voice during the election campaign. Now he knew why their political officers had been so conciliatory when the agency scriptwriters had presented such an appealing message, and had not insisted on expressing the less palatable aspects of

BNU policies.

With the issuing of the new regulations on sedition and disaffection he wondered what was next in line from the government, and when it came, a week later, it was virtually unbelievable. The House of Lords was to be abolished – there would be no second chamber and therefore no way to curb or control government excesses. The media simply noted it without comment or protest and gave no details as to what was to happen to those patriots that made up the one political sector where the BNU had little influence and no majority.

Feldt then issued a press copy of his first parliamentary statement; a statement chilling in its clarity when reported.

The United Kingdom, he said:

... is primarily an Anglo-Saxon, white Indo-European society and it would not have its ideals, culture or beliefs soiled, contaminated or corrupted by the influx of other uncivilized cultures, most of whom were diametrically opposite in religion and tradition to ours. In the past our country has given refuge to untold numbers fleeing persecution and ill-treatment. Huguenots and Palatines in the fifteenth and sixteenth centuries, Hanoverians, French Royalists, Russians, Poles and Germans in the seventeenth, eighteenth and nineteenth centuries. Even in the twentieth century we gave safe haven to Germans, Poles, Czechoslovakians, French, Dutch and later Hungarians. But these people were European, overwhelmingly Christian and with a similar culture to ours. They integrated easily and willingly into our society. And yet we are now overflowing with faces that are dissimilar to the point of being wholly foreign in religion, culture and values. They have been pandered to by a few politically powerful voices that allow the aliens' welfare to be imposed on others, in order to have their own soft and pious consciences placated.

These bleeding hearts, who have yearned for a diverse society, are condescending cowards and traitors to their heritage and, were they to hold sway, then the children of their children would live in a mixed blood society, where all that their Anglo-Saxon forebears had fought and died for would stand for nothing. These grandchildren, denied their heritage by the insidious encroachment of foreign ideals and ethnic beliefs, would spit on their grandparents' graves as they watched all our Christian churches turned into mosques.

I have nothing but contempt for the bloodless, gutless fools who would sell the country to any foreigner prepared to smile condescendingly at the British way of life, steal its wealth, and then pay a miserly sum for a house in a run-down ethnic neighbourhood; the house being large enough to accommodate a small army of a family. Why should we give refuge to a heaving mass of humanity who demand that we relinquish all that we have created and own, and offer them our heritage and wealth supposedly in the name of justice? Just because they impose on our compassion does not mean we are obliged to surrender all that we are. To often they exploit our kindness and charity and then deride it.

Appeasing those whose conscience has them ceding to Asian and black foreigners more than they will ever return to us, is pandering to folly. As Rousseau said, 'no civilized man returns good for evil or evil for good'. People who argue that we as a nation have an obligation to impoverished people on the grounds of peaceful co-existence are no less misguided; peace will not follow if we find that our indigenous population is disadvantaged because an influx of foreigners receives preferential treatment. These foreigners too quickly become parasites; parasitic in language, parasitic in education, and parasitic in culture. They take much, including our healthcare, but give very little in return.

The idea that to embrace a so-called 'diverse' society is civilized and humane is specious – to lack concern and even express favour at being swamped by other cultures, at the cost of one's own, is intolerable. It is a principle only adhered to by those too weak, fearful and insipid to uphold the supreme principle – that of advancing the culture which is their own, and is sacrificing the most. The dilution of our national culture is at risk of becoming unstoppable. While the BNU remains in power, it would no longer be the case.

It was a terrifying and alarming expression of intent, made all the more threatening when the announcement came that the government was to introduce extended terms of office – elections would now take place every ten years instead of five and during that time the political and governmental scene, both local and national, was to be frozen. There was not to be any change, so as to 'stabilize the administrative process'.

Thereafter the new laws and regulations came thick and fast. After a few half-hearted public demonstrations in which some police and the new 'public wardens' – a set of thugs hired to augment the police forces – were injured, the government announced that henceforth the police would be armed. Furthermore, to 'reduce the harm to the public being caused by anti-social elements and political extremists' the police were authorized to 'shoot on sight'. And, as the change took place, that is what many of them did. There were objections and protests of course; small groups of officers refused to accept the order, or to train with firearms, but by and large the police forces slowly emerged as a paramilitary operation. When small demonstrations occurred involving the relatives of those who had died 'in the course of a criminal act' they were rounded up and imprisoned as accomplices. Then came the 'apartheid' diktat – all marriages between Caucasian and other ethnic types were to be made null and void and where those living together refused to separate, both were at risk of being deported. Immigration was next; it was restricted to European Christians, and even then only after a strict vetting. Then came the rider to the immigration rule; new housing would be restricted to white Caucasian UK nationals, but only when the bloodline of their antecedents had been approved. These cruel orders simply added to the long list of heartless and unjust government edicts that they knew once done could not be reversed.

Mason watched with mounting apprehension as the comfortable life he knew became tainted with more and more government impositions. New laws were imposed on charities, forcing them to only provide charitable support in the UK and barring them from operating overseas – a directive that made him, and many others, shake their heads at the pettiness of it. Worse was to come when all strikes and public demonstrations were outlawed and it was obvious to everyone that the country was now a one-party state, governed by contemptible and dogmatic ideologists whose creed was 'we know best and we will retain power at all costs'.

National Service came about five months into the BNU's administration. It was announced, so it was said, for reasons of international security. The government's overseas aid and welfare fund was to be cancelled and the money diverted to military acquisitions. It had been agreed, the MOD said, with all NATO members, that in the event of an international crisis the UK would be able to field at least seven infantry combat divisions with four in reserve, as well as five full armoured divisions and supporting artillery. The air force and the navy were also to be significantly increased. All men, and certain female specialists, between the ages of eighteen and twenty-seven were liable. Of course, taxation was hoisted to pay for it all. This was the one pre-election aspect everyone knew about, but not the 3 per cent it turned out to be.

Like before, there was little in the way of protest and where it did happen the so-called 'malcontents' were quickly dispersed or imprisoned. Mason tried to keep everything in the agency on a normal footing, but the atmosphere degraded rapidly from an all-pervading sense of intimidation to that of living in a condemned cell. As yet, the agency and its staff appeared to be inviolate as far as any direct impingement on their activities or freedom of movement, but the agency's tense atmosphere signalled that it was only a matter of time before the government applied a stranglehold one way or another.

As matters deteriorated he could see the writing on the wall. Margaret's mood started to become prickly and short tempered. Their trips home in the evening to their new apartment in Borehamwood started to become an ordeal. Too often, while leaving the agency, they could see across the Thames to Brixton and other ethnic sectors in London, with the relevant horizon lit up from the glow of huge fires as another anti-government demonstration turned into riot and violent mayhem.

He had long despaired that the subliminal imprinting would by now have begun to abate. He remembered Emma Lilton's jottings that Sam Taylor had given him, and he clung on to Lilton's and Armstrong's opinion that the imprinting should weaken after a period of time. However, it had not been systematically followed up as yet, and all the evidence so far was that the imprinting did not fade, or if it did, it was a very slow process. The BNU broadcasts had been more heavily delta modulated; perhaps that explained the slow abatement.

His despondent and near-devastated frame of mind was made all the worse by his ever-deepening sense of shame and guilt and, for all his insightful ability, he could see no immediate way of salvaging the situation or of salving his conscience. Worse was the fact that as his remorse gave way to a determination to remedy his past mistakes, the Ministry of Home Affairs gave notice that all mosques were to be demolished and that mass deportation of Muslim clerics was to begin. Sharia law and all councils were immediately outlawed – anyone convicted of participation faced dire penalties, including deportation. Border controls were to be tightened further; even British passport-holders would be refused re-entry if they were suspected of ethnic sympathies. To his surprise there was nothing as yet demonstrating anti-Semitic policies. That, he supposed would follow – perhaps more subtly to avoid international condemnation. The BNU seemed to know that they could go so far and no further.

In terms of his own situation and that of his staff, he observed relatively little as a consequence of the creeping impact of the new policies – apart from a pervading sense of anxiety it engendered. It left him and his staff untouched and seemingly indifferent, other than to underline how danger-ous the new administration was. It was as though they were a protected entity – perhaps they were, having acquired a special status. As he thought about it, he realized that he, like others, was becoming inured to successive government attacks on the long-cherished tradition of democratic and religious freedom.

In truth, mere shame, guilt and resentment was not a propitious start to his portrayal as a resistance fighter; but at least he had made his choice. He was primarily responsible for the BNU gaining power – now he had to be the one that took it away from them. The question was... how?

Chapter 22

AN OPPORTUNITY TO reverse the mess his earlier avarice
had fashioned came unexpectedly; it was an opportunity far from his thoughts, but one he could not forego.

Margaret had given him a ninety-minute diary appointment for two days hence, highlighting the fact that it was
to be with the BNU again. Middleton, the deputy prime
minister, was due with two other ministers, Benson and
Frobisher. As usual she made no comment on the prospects
for the meeting, but he knew that she would be aware that
his rising resentment was likely to make it a difficult encounter, whatever the subject. He'd made no effort in Margaret's
presence to hide his sense of guilt or his mounting animosity
towards the BNU and its policies. She, in turn, had tried to
placate his bitterness by reminding him that it hadn't been
for purely personal reasons he'd accepted the BNU contract.
The agency staff, she reminded him, had nearly all been his
collaborators in the rise to power by the BNU – once they
knew what the rewards were, their morality had submerged
without trace.

What she said was true, but it was hardly therapeutic as
far as his feelings were concerned. And yet the forthcoming
meeting had to be endured and handled diplomatically. A lot
depended on it; he would do well not to alienate the BNU

party bosses. On the contrary, if he played the game sensibly and tactically, he might learn enough to make his heartfelt wish come true.

They filed in to his office on time; a smiling trio with Middleton in the lead and Benson and Frobisher lagging slightly behind; three charming sharks.

Strange it might be, but he found no difficulty in presenting a pleasant and pleasurable face as they arrived, and it was only as he reminded himself that these three affable men were primarily responsible for the darkness and disruption the country was experiencing that it all seemed so incongruous. Facing them across his desk a sense of cold resolve came to him and his feeling of trepidation vanished.

As they found seats in front of his desk Margaret brought in trays of coffee and biscuits. Her timing and proficiency was perfect; she was on cue and with no sense of haste, eventually attracting generous expressions of thanks. If nothing else, they gave the impression of being decent and appreciative gentlemen.

With the coffee distributed, he heard Benson lean over to Middleton and say, 'This is where it all started, Elliot made it happen.' Middleton nodded in agreement and took a sip from his coffee.

'Well gentlemen, to what do I owe the pleasure? Don't tell me you intend to hold another general election.'

The quip was taken in the spirit in which it was intended and they all laughed. It was a risk, but he'd avoided any offence.

Indeed, Frobisher was thoroughly tickled by his remark and was the last to control his laughter. Red of face he finally spoke. 'You don't have to worry about that Elliot, not for at least ten years.'

As this was said Benson lifted a hand to prevent Frobisher

from diverting the conversation away from their proposed route.

Benson pointed at Middleton. 'The DPM here has taken the view that our policies are causing some alienation amongst the people. We need to explain to them what we are doing and why... so as to counter the growing hostility – a hostility even amongst our own rank and file I might add. We believe that a few well-timed public information broadcasts will bring the sheep back into the fold so to speak, and we would like you to arrange it.'

Middleton stepped in. 'As I understand it, Elliot, I hope you won't mind the familiarity, you have the secret of highly effective political productions, and we want you to repeat the success you demonstrated in our party political broadcasts over the election period. Being sympathetic to our cause, I assume you have no objections.'

At first a feeling of entrapment came over him. Being sympathetic to their cause was not as he saw it, and after Middleton's comments he was disposed to the idea that they might want to add him to their party membership.

God forbid.

He was being cornered into fostering and supporting the very thing he was trying to dismantle. Where would this take him? Perhaps a little frank talking might clarify matters.

'Let's call a spade a spade, gentlemen. You speak of public information broadcasts, but what we are really talking about is propaganda... are we not? The truth is that any production that justifies current government decisions, and is persuasive enough to appease or sway discontented citizens, is propaganda. Now, I personally don't care what label is stuck on it – just so I am clear about what content you want and what kind of contract will follow. After all, this agency needs to survive financially, if only to cater to the BNU!'

The three turned and smiled at each other, satisfied with his response.

Frobisher was the first to speak. 'Quite right, Elliot. We would like to arrange things as we did before – our party political officers will liaise with your production staff for three video presentations. However, this time we want a wider series of posters to be designed for national dissemination so I imagine all your graphics people will be involved. We would like to see all of this ready within eight weeks. Can it be done... and how much?'

He sat back in his chair working out the logistics of the proposal and totalling up the costs.

'I can't be certain at this stage but my gut feeling is that we are talking about thirty-five million. It could be less but I suspect not. If that is too much we may have to cut our cloth a different way.'

Frobisher shook his head. 'We have more than enough in the way of resources to meet that figure. Our sponsors and the treasury have deep pockets.'

He smiled back at them. 'Are you not concerned that the electoral commission might not want to know who is backing the BNU, and from whom you are getting sponsorship money? Surely, given the figures we have discussed, it can't all be declared as legitimate funds.'

Benson waved a dismissive hand. 'The electoral commission is now defunct – it is no longer necessary. We abolished it directly we took over.'

He was again astonished – this was yet another hammer blow against real parliamentary democracy.

'Well... good... that there is no chance of any official enquiries; I take it then that the thirty-five million can be committed.'

'And what about yourself, Elliot, was that fee you've just mentioned inclusive?' Middleton had given him an intent look and a somewhat sardonic smile.

It had no effect – he had already decided that his best strategy was to inculcate himself into their good graces.

'Oh! You mistake me, gentlemen! I seem to have been well rewarded already. I think you can discount any further outlays other than the agency fee I have just referred to. I imagine that will demonstrate my sincerity.'

Benson piped up, 'It was never in doubt, Elliot, we have great faith in what you can do for us. *À propos* that, we will need to include some very sensitive material in the... er... new productions. We want to convey to the electorate that our policies and the subsequent recent changes to law, and the augmenting of the civil authorities, are in the best interests of the people of Britain. Likewise, we need to drive home the fact that much of what has transpired since we took office is for the general good of the country; that we maintain employment, that civil rights are guarded by a far more effective police force, and that regardless of international criticism, we are giving the country back to the indigenous population.'

Middleton added his voice. 'More than that, we have the economy under control, exports are rising – particularly in arms sales – and the standard of living is improving day on day. We know full well that there is a small clutch of reactionaries who trigger demonstrations and create civil unrest, but they will be dealt with. It will only be a short time, once we settle matters, before we are seen to be the principled and altruistic administration we feel we are.'

Listening to the obnoxious and disingenuous tripe emanating from the two BNU men, he suddenly had a thought.

'As a matter of interest, what has the King to say about the current situation?'

Frobisher gave an embarrassed giggle while Benson took on a smirk.

'His Majesty is resting – we decided that given the King's state of health and his mother's advanced age, it would be better if he and his family remained at Balmoral until the political climate cooled. It would be upsetting and inappropriate for their Majesties to be close to any unrest.'

As Benson became silent, Mason simply nodded his head and jotted a few pointless remarks on his notepad. It was intended to appear as though he was making observations or comments on the meeting. In fact there was no need.

'Good! Gentlemen, I have your verbal expressions of interest, if there is nothing else, I will arrange contracts to be forwarded to your office, Deputy Prime Minister, and we will begin work sometime later this week. I trust—'

Frobisher interrupted with, 'One moment Elliot we—'

Frobisher in turn was then over-talked into silence by Middleton.

'Elliot, one other thing – we would like what you produce for us to be privately screened before it has a public viewing. The PM has taken the view that all parliamentary BNU members and party officers should have the option to appraise and evaluate the content of the programmes. Just to ensure everyone agrees with what they see and, where appropriate, to make suggestions for material to be included or deleted. I'm sure you see the sense in that. Of course, the version for general appraisal would need to be a virgin version – no special additions.'

For a second or two his whole being leaped; he instantly saw what he had been looking for and here it was – a complete gift.

'Yes, of course – a private screening. Understood.'

He gave the three men a sincere and joyful smile – he had the trap, but how to spring it?

'OK my friends – I will start this project asap. I will look forward to your people coming in and enjoying the same welcome as before and as warm a working relationship as last time. I'm sure you will get what you want. That said, I wish you all a good day.'

They all shook hands and it was patently clear that the three were confident of their success in their objectives. As they filed out, again with Middleton at the head, he heard them offer Margaret the usual pleasantries. She replied happily that she hoped they would all have a productive day. Not one failed to say that they thought otherwise.

A little later Margaret brought him a coffee. He kissed her and held her hand as he gave her a synopsis of the meeting.

'I've just shaken hands with three people who make my flesh crawl. Perhaps that makes me a hypocrite but that's how I feel these days. Just for a second back there I thought they were going to offer me an honourary party member- ship. Imagine how difficult it would have been to deflect it. I'm glad to say it didn't materialize.'

Margaret grinned. 'And yet you look very pleased with yourself; I thought that you would come out of it more depressed than before. What's changed? Don't tell me that your list of public enemies has been revised by meeting those three.'

'No – quite the reverse, a more malignant, hypocritical, autocratic if not tyrannical bunch it would be hard to find. Thank God the meeting only lasted thirty minutes, had it been the full ninety I think I would have given up the will to live. But they have given me an opportunity, one too good to ignore.'

'Tell me – what opportunity? For what?'

'I can't tell you yet – but I will, I promise. First I need Nigel Armstrong and Simon Rogers here; see if you can find them. I know we have a contact number for Simon and with luck he will know where Nigel is. Follow it up, sweetie, see what you can do – it's very important.'

Chapter 23

Simon found his Shropshire home environment ideal for writing up the final sections of his thesis. The slow pace of village life, offering peace and solitude, not to mention the lack of interruptions and distractions from his fellow students, gave him freedom and respite, and enabled him to concentrate on writing a well-balanced text.

It had been a fraught and interminable journey from London to Shrewsbury and he had only begun to relax as the taxi sped its way through the open countryside to his parents' village. Here the population was sparse, and it was a relief to note the complete absence of armed police. Even now he shuddered when he remembered the way the police and the so-called public wardens kept watch at the stations, and how they bullied the many vagrants that now congregated around the warmer or more sheltered areas. Whole families huddled together, starving and without hope, as the government callously dismantled the welfare safety net. It was clear that the country was limping back to a social and economic structure that a mid-Victorian would have recognized. The dispossessed were now a common sight and their haunted faces spoke volumes.

He, of course, was spared any adversity. Received with joy on his arrival, his mother and father gave their all to ensure he continued to aspire to his dreamed-of status. As he immersed himself in his thesis his parents, proud of his intellectual abilities, had stood back admiringly and let him get on with it. It allowed him to think and organize. The jumble of three years' worth of coding, and the justification of all the sub-routines, slipped into place with hardly any effort. Jeffrey Innes had already seen an earlier draft and had sent him three A4 pages dense with corrections, revisions and amendments. But it was all done. Now he was very close to finalizing the last draft and on the day he hit the last keyboard letter, it was with a deep sense of release.

The final version would go out to Jeffrey by email and he would then have to await the imminent date for his viva voce at UCL – the last hurdle.

In the last analysis he had no need to complete his PhD, he was a wealthy man and could probably live comfortably for the rest of his life. But he was reluctant to abandon all his training and interest; to do so would make him feel guilty. It struck him as a terrible waste – and what would he do with his time?

His parents were still unaware of his financial state. Explaining to his conservative mother and father how he had come by his riches would be seriously problematic. He knew it would shame him and likely spark off a confrontation. He intended to reward them later, at the appropriate moment – as soon as he could justify his newfound wealth, that was. For the interim he contributed to his mother's housekeeping and pretended moderate hardship. Not only did he want to justify any reward for his loving parents, he had to think about his future – academic or otherwise.

It was as he returned home in the late afternoon that his mother told him that there had been a phone call from a Margaret Delaney. His mother thought it was a mistake when Ms Delaney had told her that she was calling from an advertising agency called Morley, Swan & Bramly. But no, apparently there was no mistake! Ms Delaney definitely wanted to speak to Simon Rogers.

His mother seemed aghast that a call from an advertising agency should be directed at her son – it was far from the elitist gatherings she expected. He managed to soothe her rather theatrical distress by pointing out that MS&B were linked to the college, and it was all to do with a college-wide charity drive. MS&B, he told her, had agreed to be sponsors.

With his mother now placated he looked at the telephone number that she had jotted down earlier and then glanced at the hallway clock – it was ten to five – early enough. He rang the number.

The voice that answered he recognized – it was Elliot Mason's secretary.

'Ms Delaney, this is Simon Rogers – you tried to contact me earlier.'

'Yes I did Simon, I'm very glad to hear from you. Do you think you could be present at a meeting with Elliot Mason sometime next week? And do you have a contact telephone number or address for Nigel Armstrong?'

As the questions arose he realized that he was unlikely to make London the following week but he did have Nigel's mobile number.

'Ms Delaney...'

'Margaret, please.'

'Oh... yes of course. Well, I'm sorry... I can't make next week Margaret but my viva is being arranged for the week after next at UCL so I will be in London Monday fortnight. As for Nigel, I can give you a mobile number but contact may be difficult. I believe he's in the Orkney Islands – a village called Balfour on an island called... er... Shapinsay if I recall correctly. I've had no contact from him, or reason to make contact with him, for a long time now so I can't say if he is still there. If he is answering his mobile you'll soon know where he is.'

He heard a slight exclamation of incredulity.

'Did you say Shapinsay in the Orkneys?'

'Yes, he left the university just after his final meeting with Elliot. He told me he was leaving because he had a book to write and needed time to overcome some personal disappointment.'

There was silence for a moment.

'I see. What is the date of your viva Simon – can I arrange something a few days before?'

'I don't see why not – my viva is scheduled for the Thursday two weeks hence. I suppose I could be with you on the Tuesday.'

'OK Simon, we'll make it the Tuesday – that's the eighteenth. Now, a favour please. I know you have Nigel Armstrong's mobile number? Would you try to contact him on my behalf? I know this may seem strange, and an inconvenience, but I assure you there is a very good reason for my request. If you do make contact, ask him if he can make the London appointment on the eighteenth. Please tell him it's important.'

For a moment he was puzzled, but decided Margaret's appeal was a minor inconvenience.

'OK Margaret, I'll do what I can to coax him away from his solitude – wherever it might be. I'll let you know.'

'Many thanks, Simon – look forward to seeing you on the eighteenth. Bye.'

As he was listening to Margaret, it occurred to him that if Elliot Mason had called a meeting between Mason, Nigel and a certain Simon Rogers, then it must be something important.

All being well, he would find out on the eighteenth.

This was the third attempt to get a response from Nigel Armstrong's mobile. Every previous attempt had ended with the ring tone being cancelled and him being deafened by an empty, but noisy, line. He blamed his own mobile phone to some extent; it was ancient, but even with his new wealth it never occurred to buy another.

He was about to ring off when he heard the line open and a voice said, 'Hello Simon – how are you these days?'

'Ah, Nigel, can't tell you how glad I am to hear your voice. I'm well thank you, and you?'

'Well enough thanks, to what do I owe the pleasure of your dulcet tones?'

He decided on a diplomatic response.

'I had a call from Elliot Mason. He's asking for a meeting at the agency on the eighteenth of this month. He wants us both to attend; I can... can you?'

'I could if I were to fly down, but I'm not inclined to do so. I'm busy and it could be a two-day round trip – a waste of two days.'

For a moment he didn't know how to respond.

'Nigel, are you still in the Orkneys?'

'I am – and what is more I like it up here. I moved from Shapinsay to Kirkwell recently – nice people, very civilized.'

'Well, that makes life difficult, Elliot seems to think it's important we get together.'

'Does he? Well, I'm disinclined to travel but it's the modern world now. Tell him I'm perfectly happy to make contact via a video link using Skype. You and he can be on the London side, I can remain up here – though for the life of me I can't see what he needs us for anymore.'

'Are you equipped to make the link - have you done it before?'

'I have, it's no problem, just get me his Skype registration, email or phone number and a time for the link. OK?'

'Yeah sure, I look forward to seeing you again, even if it's only on screen.'

'Yeah – incidentally, how's the thesis coming along?'

'Hah. My viva is two days after the meeting with Mason. I've got my fingers tightly crossed.'

'Uncross them, you'll walk it I'm sure.'

He smiled, grateful for the typical Armstrong encouragement.

'Thanks, Nigel – I'll be in touch soon. Stay by your phone. I'll speak to you soon. Take care.'

'You too, Simon. Bye.'

As he hit the cancel button on his phone he wondered why Nigel, a wealthy man, would not simply charter a plane, speed to the meeting after landing at London, and be back in the air heading for the Orkneys an hour or two later. There had to be a reason, but it was not his business. He let it go. Tomorrow he would meet his obligations regarding contact with Nigel and then look forward to his final few weeks in London – never to return.

Chapter 24

THEY HAD SET up the video link in Mason's office. There were three of them around the screen; Mason, Rogers and Sam Taylor. Margaret had been told to lock her outside door and the connecting door between her office and Elliot Mason's.

The arrangement was that Nigel Armstrong would come on line at 3 p.m. and they waited patiently for the first picture to arrive. Four flasks of coffee and tea had been set up to one side of the office and in a slightly tense atmosphere, each man silently refilled his cup as they all waited. Then Nigel Armstrong suddenly appeared on screen.

'Hello everyone – I trust you are receiving me – can you please shift your webcam to the left so that... ah, thank you.'

Sam Taylor had moved forward as the request came in and it was clear everyone was now in shot.

'Good, spot on – hello Elliot, Roger, Sam – not quite the Three Musketeers, and unfortunately I'm not D'Artagnan, but nevertheless, I imagine this meeting is to do with something far more important than the Queen's diamonds.'

'In a sense, Nigel – Dumas' story was about efforts to ensure a state would not be overthrown by a tyrant; this is about removing a tyrant from an already overthrown one.

As Mason spoke the two others looked at the screen, trying to see whether Armstrong understood Mason's cryptic statement.

For a moment Armstrong said nothing and then he shrugged.

'Fair enough – back to how it was before the BNU got in – why am I so important?'

Mason leaned forward as if in a confidential huddle.

'Because I need to ask you a simple question, Nigel, one I believe only you can answer, but I can't give you the full context as yet. All you need to do today is give us your expert opinion on the query and then we are done.'

There was a perceptible hesitation and then; 'OK – fire away.'

'What level of delta modulation would, or could, make the imprinting lethal?'

Nigel Armstrong gave a shocked look.

'Why – are imprinted people dying?'

'No, quite the opposite, the last exposure appears to be taking a very long time to abate.'

Armstrong gave a slight nod of his head.

'Well, the increased modulation we last used may account for that but I believe, as Emma Lilton did, that it will fade in time. Looking at her experimental notes, as I did when I was last at UCL, she thought the imprinting effect was exponential – so even a small increase in modulation would have a profound effect on the subject.'

Mason nodded too.

'So, it is likely to stay with a subject for some considerable time. That is becoming clear. But I want you to consider my first question – how could it become lethal?'

Again, Nigel Armstrong looked momentarily blank.

'I really can't say offhand. We know that subjects under hypnosis cannot be instructed to commit suicide or do anything their subconscious will rejects. But then again, subliminal isn't strictly hypnosis – not in the conventional sense. All I can say is that with sufficient delta modulation, and an appropriate visual stimulus, it might be possible to instil a lethal command. I suppose that if you ran an apparently innocuous visual programme and then interposed very brief and imperceptible messages, just as the old idea of subliminal imprinting was used, you might get the desired effect.'

For a moment there was silence as Armstrong finished. Then Sam Taylor raised a hand.

'Yeah, Sam, how can I help?'

'Listen Nigel, if I am to understand you we simply insert messages into the programme on view which instruct the subject to take lethal action – is that it? So what would these messages say? How do you convince someone that they should ignore any fundamental, subconscious will of self-preservation?'

'Not easy – the message has to invite them to do something that offers a better option – a message that says "death is the right thing to do". Come to think of it, that message would probably work. It has to be something that does not impart fear, rather it offers forgiveness or a kind of paradise; something like that. I—'

Mason interjected. 'What's your gut feeling on the likelihood of it working, Nigel? Would you lay bets?'

Armstrong's head leaned back and he studied whatever it was above him.

'I would take a two-to-one bet in favour. My guess is that it will probably work on most subjects with the right level of delta modulation. Get the message right and it should be effective. However, the message is the thing, and I can't be definite about how persuasive one message might be against another. However, I will think on that and come back to you.'

Mason nodded his appreciation. 'Thank you Nigel, I'll look forward to hearing from you. You have my email address, don't you? Before you go, our apologies again for not revealing the full picture. The less you know the better, I'm sure you understand.'

Armstrong gave a broad smile.

'Thanks Elliot, but I'm not that imperceptive – were I really that dim-witted you wouldn't be consulting me. I wish you well; I know what you hope to do so good luck, I'll be in touch. One last thing – please pass on my regards to Margaret. Tell her I wish her happiness.'

The screen went blank, and a white static loaded picture replaced the smiling face of Nigel Armstrong.

Elliot Mason was left looking at the blank screen wondering if Nigel Armstrong had any inkling about Margaret and himself. It didn't appear so, and for that he was grateful. As things stood he had no idea how he might broach the subject with Armstrong. He hoped he would never need to.

He turned back to his two guests.

'If either of you have any questions I'd like to hear them now. We've already discussed what needs to be done, and by the time the BNU so-called public information productions are complete we must still be determined and able to carry out our plan. If any of you have reservations I need to know.'

Sam Taylor came forward and sat down in front of Mason's desk.

'We are proposing to assassinate the whole of the current executive and the BNU hierarchy. Personally I have no objections; my only doubts are to do with what comes after. You can be sure it will be chaos and anarchy – how exactly do you return a country to normality after such an act, and for the duration of what will be a complete breakdown in public order?'

Mason moved forward and sat down behind his desk.

'We have about seven weeks to plan for that, but in truth it is the lesser of our problems. We'll cross that bridge when we get to it. Now, questions and gripes please.'

Neither Taylor nor Rogers spoke.

Mason looked at Simon Rogers, the most modest of his three co-conspirators, but even at his youthful age, of immense integrity.

'Simon, you've remained very laconic since we met. Have I your undertaking that you will stay with the plan for as long as it takes?'

Rogers remembered all that he had seen on his travels – the evicted and starving families, the brutal police stop-and-search episodes, the fear that his little village and his family would ultimately be invaded by this odious and detestable administration. Oh yes, he would stay.

'Certainly Elliot, whatever needs to be done I will do. I will ensure I am available whenever you require me. Sam and I will confer on the delta modulation process and anything else Nigel contributes. My viva is on Thursday – after that I'm all yours.'

Mason gave a grim smile.

'Good – that's it then and good luck Simon. I'll await the result with interest.'

He stood and shook hands with his co-conspirators, inwardly praying that what they intended to do would bring an end to what had blighted the country. He had provided the initial machinery and was thus an instigator; he now intended to be the terminator.

The State Interception and Surveillance Team was now part of the Government Communications Headquarters and had been set up in haste. They were only just becoming confident that they could adequately intercept any communication that took place through UK servers and telephone exchanges. Their new computer system was programmed to listen for key words that might indicate subversion or anti-government conspiracies. Its immensely fast-time division monitoring technology instantly scrutinized all national communications, and printed out the source, recipient and context the moment it detected what had been identified as 'subversive' terms.

It was, however, invariably a boring activity for the human operators who realized that it was not necessarily the word that might point to any treason, subversion or rebellion but the context. Words such as 'kill', 'politically inept', 'autocratic', 'hateful', 'bomb', 'secret', 'minister', 'despotic', 'ruthless' or 'malignant' were very seldom in the context of a conspiracy or indicating some plan to do harm to the state. Furthermore, when the system threw up words or phrases it failed to comprehend, the human operators often had the opportunity to laugh with the old maxim 'to err is human, to really screw up you need a computer'.

So it was that a few hours after Elliot Mason's group and Nigel Armstrong had finished their Skype exchange, a SIST operator was momentarily puzzled by the interception computer's report that during a video link it had failed to identify certain phrases and words. One was 'overthrown by a tyrant' – 'state' had been noted as too 'subliminal' – also 'modulation', 'BNU' and 'lethal'.

The operator was unsure of what 'subliminal' and 'modulation' meant and the other words were all too common to necessarily indicate a plot. As far as the two key words were concerned, it was too close to her lunch break to call up the internet and find out their meaning.

As the thought of food occurred, she felt her stomach rumble in expectation of her lunchtime sandwiches. It was too tempting, and something she would not delay in getting to or consuming.

She gave the printout one more look and made her decision.

She turned, levelled the sheet, and pushed it into the mouth of the nearby shredder. As the cutters tore into the paper, she backed away, picked up her lunch box, and made her way to the canteen.

Chapter 25

THIS TIME IT was different. He detected a sullen if not brooding atmosphere as the various teams working on the government public information programmes engaged with their unwelcome obligation.

The BNU electoral programmes had been a source of pride and at the time they had been carried out, it had taken place in a cooperative atmosphere. But the difference between then and now was the fact that his staff had already tasted the kind of overbearing government their previous work had guided into power, and they didn't like it. To now find themselves working to aid the continuance of an administration they detested made for a very strained working environment.

The BNU officers were the same faces as before, only this time they were far more insistent that the content of the programmes should only follow their script and agenda. It was clear that they had received instructions not to allow the agency scriptwriters to determine, or intervene, on what was to be said, nor how it should be said.

Slowly he became aware of the escalating hostility between staff and the BNU and it made him apprehensive. He could not afford to allow matters to deteriorate to the point where open disputes broke out. Even with the promise of a second round of staff bonuses, it could easily become the case that staff would disregard their payments if, and when, clashes occurred. He couldn't be sure, but he was beginning to see a change in his people; the passive mood that most displayed after the electoral imprinting was starting to disappear. That too was a danger – disputes disrupted progress; if programmes were compromised it would have enormous consequences for his plans.

That evening he waited until the BNU people had left for home having had Sam Taylor tell all MS&B staff to remain behind. He called them into the canteen and when they were assembled, he made a short speech.

It was from the heart.

'You may be hostile to what you are being asked to do but don't rock the boat. Don't antagonize the BNU people. Demonstrate your professionalism and make the programmes and posters as well as you might for a corporate assignment. Trust me, there is too much at stake for anyone to disrupt or damage the current series of projects. If it happens everyone will pay for it, not just one individual. Tomorrow I want to see full cooperation with the BNU officers – what they want, they get. Is that understood?'

It wasn't exactly a full-blown accord, but there were no dissenting voices.

As they all filed out Sam Taylor caught his eye and winked. It was reassuring – perhaps he had prevented a mutiny for the interim, but he had better keep a close surveillance on all and sundry. As things stood, his people were likely to become their own worst enemies.

Three weeks into the second agency engagement with the BNU he was becoming a little less anxious. Even Margaret had noticed the calm, if not subdued environment that pervaded the work floors. He was now only concerned about one thing – Nigel Armstrong had not, as yet, made contact.

He was tempted to make contact himself but then realized he wasn't able to. Simon Rogers had not passed over the contact telephone number for Nigel and although Nigel had the agency's contact details, the reverse was not true. The only thing he could do was to get Margaret to contact Simon Rogers and start the original process over again.

He was about to get Margaret to start when she came in to his office.

'Just got a call from Simon Rogers. He's back home in Shropshire. His PhD viva was successful – hopes you'll be pleased. He told me he was contacted by Nigel Armstrong yesterday and has some information for you. He's going to email it to you. Apparently Nigel was very reluctant to phone here at the agency and he hasn't got your email address. Thought it simpler to have Simon pass on his message. I do feel for Nigel, he is a nice man and I think I hurt him a lot. I do hope he finds someone else.'

He listened with a combination of elation and sympathy – yes, Nigel was a nice man, but the truth was he was glad he had abandoned the competition over Margaret.

'OK darling – glad about Simon and glad to know I love a woman who has empathy in her soul. I'll wait for the email, I just hope Simon isn't too distracted to send it.'

She smiled at his remarks. 'Thank you for that and I don't think Simon will forget – I reminded him that it was important. He said he had nothing else to think about for the moment so it wasn't likely he would overlook it.'

'Great – so we wait. By the by, what do you fancy for dinner tonight – a takeaway?'

He saw her lovely face break into a bigger smile. 'Oh, yes but perhaps we could try to find a restaurant – I have a penchant for a curry... no, on second thoughts, they've all shut down. I suppose it will have to be fish and chips. Damn, I'll cook, Elliot, it's safer.'

He came towards her and gave her a kiss.

'No – we'll find a restaurant, wherever we can find one open, and see what's on the menu... it'll save you cooking. Tonight we dine à la carte.'

Suddenly there was a bleep on his PC.

'See,' Margaret quipped, 'I told you Simon wouldn't forget.'

He looked at the message and its propositions for the umpteenth time. It was clear that Nigel had applied some contorted thinking to the problem. If no one abreast of what they were trying to do had seen each of Nigel's suggestions, it could only be concluded that they had originated in a deeply perverse and morbid mind. And yet there must have been a great deal of agonizing about what was most likely to have the desired effect. His first offer was nearly the same as he had originally proposed:

'Death is the moral thing to do.'

Then came:

'Living cannot make you better – end your life.'

Followed by:

'All your wrongs terminate with death – end life now.'

Finally he suggested:

'Your existence is futile – stop your life being pointless.'

Which, he remarked, was probably the most likely to appeal to those already clinically depressed. His comment, that he could not guarantee which would have the greater impact, was followed by the idea that if the video programme were extensive, then including each and every one of the subliminal messages over the duration of the programme would eliminate risking only the weakest.

It made sense, and he printed out the email, consigning it

to his private desk drawer. The next thing to do was to get Sam and Simon together long enough to be able to compose and carry out the visual and delta wave insertions on the BNU programmes. Then they were to await the preview of the programmes by the BNU hierarchy. They would assume the programmes were virgin – they were in for a shock.

Chapter 26

MUCH AGAINST HIS will, he watched the final versions of each of the three BNU public information programmes and examined all the poster artwork.

This time all of it was highly nationalistic, typical of a malignant despotic regime that used semantic ambiguity to reinforce its ideology. The people's party, one read, provided 'popular enlightenment'. Another spoke of removing 'archaic political repression under previous governments', of 'cultural identity' being at the heart of 'patriotism' thus enabling the people to become 'liberated' by dint of 'true democracy'. The economic situation was under control and adjusted to give 'maximum shared surplus' among workers and to ensure 'minimum unemployment'. He almost laughed – you only had to go out on the streets to see how disingenuous the last claim was. Even the video presentations, smooth and appealing but glorifying the current power base, were reminiscent of the triumphant propaganda typical of Nazi Germany in the 1930s.

Every viewing he took depressed him further, but he was obliged to make serious comments and frequently murmur approval because, as he toured the work floor, he was flanked by the three BNU officers, who were all clearly very proud of the material on show.

As the last video closed, he turned to the three. 'Well gentlemen, I can only offer my sincere thanks for your insightful contribution to the material I've just seen. I was confident that it would all resolve satisfactorily and so it has. I now need to notify our principals to arrange the full party review, which I suspect will be met with no little enthusiasm. I will of course pass on to your minister my high regard and sincere admiration for the way you have integrated with my people and for your perceptive and knowledgeable contribution. I'm sure it will be recognized at a higher level.'

They all smiled ingratiatingly, intimating thanks and appreciation. He was about to take his leave when one of them said, 'Mr Mason, it appears that the scrutiny of our work by all the senior party members has been arranged to take place in Westminster Hall on the parliamentary estate. We were told that with the completion of the video programmes well ahead of schedule, they have decided to screen everything as soon as possible. We think that means within the next ten days – just as soon as they can fit the necessary chairs, screens and video projection equipment. It should be quite a show. A ministerial confirmation for you to forward all the completed material is on its way.'

For a moment he was speechless, it meant he had to get Sam Taylor and Simon Rogers together as soon as possible to carry out the subliminal insertions and apply the delta modulation. He hoped that the fleeting look of shock he gave had not been too obvious to the three around him.

'That's encouraging – we'll have to move quickly to refine the titles and credits for the videos – naturally you three will be fully recognized in the programme credits. Now, is there anything else we need to do?'

His query was met with silence and a few gently shaken heads.

'Very well then, I look forward to seeing you all in Westminster Hall. Take care on the way back to your offices.'

As he shook hands he felt relief that hopefully this was the last time he would encounter these political pawns. If all went according to plan, he would soon be attending their funerals.

Margaret made contact with Simon Rogers three hours later inviting him back to London to meet Elliot Mason and Sam Taylor.

'I know you are back home, Simon, but Elliot needs a group meeting to thrash out an urgent problem. Can you make it in the next thirty-six hours?'

Simon kept silent and then said, 'Yes, I'll fly down. I'll get a charter flight from Birmingham. I should be with you tomorrow morning all being well. Tell Elliot that contrary to what I said before, I can't keep making London appointments, I don't travel well – next time he'll have to meet me at least halfway.'

Margaret didn't know whether to laugh or sympathize with his last remark; she'd heard that Simon became anxious when on his travels. Nigel had said Simon always travelled with a friend, one called 'trepidation'.

'OK Simon, I will pass on the message. If I may say so, it could well be that after this appointment there will be no more need for you to make a trip. Fingers crossed.'

'Perhaps, I hope so. Thank you Margaret, I look forward to seeing you soon.'

As the connection to Simon Rogers was cut, she immediately dialled Sam Taylor's internal number. At first no one picked up the phone then a female voice said 'Samantha, CGI desk.'

'Is Sam with you, Samantha?'

'No, he's patching some video at the moment on the video

editing desk. Shall I ask him to phone you?'

'No – just ask him to make his way to Mr Mason's office as soon as possible. He wants a chinwag. OK?'

'No problem.'

Sam Taylor gave a quick knock on his office door and then virtually burst in.

'Elliot, hello – what's the emergency?'

He opened the intercom. 'Margaret, lock your office door and mine please.'

As he received her acknowledgment he waved Sam into a chair to the front of his desk, but was already briefing him before the man had even sat down.

'Listen Sam, you and Simon have an urgent task ahead. I understand that the BNU parliamentary party, their constituency agents, sponsors and hangers-on are intending to have a showing in Westminster Hall of the so-called public info stuff we have just completed. That's some ten days from now. We have to get copies of the video presentations doctored and slipped into the programme within that time. Now, we are going to do something suggested by Nigel Armstrong and that is to insert four subliminal messages into the video programme itself and not simply depend on just one; nor just the delta wave imprinting. Here, read this and tell me what you think.'

He unlocked his private drawer extracting the copy of the email from Armstrong and handed it over to Taylor.

Sam Taylor began to read and almost instantly the colour started to drain from his face. He scanned the whole thing again and then dropped the arm holding the email until it lay limply on the armrest of the chair.

'Christ almighty Elliot – Nigel has really done one hell of a job on this. I hope it's not a joke.'

He gave Taylor a penetrating look.

'Would he joke about it? I don't think so.'

Taylor gave a shrug.

'Fairly cold and calculating though, he's certainly taking a somewhat indifferent view to mass murder.'

'He knows what's at stake – how else do you suggest we eliminate a political affliction? They've got an iniquitous and vice-like grip on the country; we've been given a way to remove it. If you now think you've no stomach for it, or are squeamish in any way, say so.'

Taylor licked his lips.

'You ask if I'm squeamish? No… I knew what we were intending to do during the video link with Nigel, but seeing these sinister messages in stark black and white is a touch unsettling. However, it changes nothing, it's a means to an end; the insertions will be done and I'll do them.'

'Good, Simon will be here tomorrow to help with the delta modulation, no doubt you will—'

'I don't need Simon's help – I can do all that needs to be done myself. Our video editing desk is ideal for the job; it still has the add-ons that the previous consultants were using. I've been practising what Simon and Nigel taught me and I'm confident I know what I'm doing. If Simon is travelling down you might want to postpone his arrival.'

He gave the remark some thought. Better he depended on Sam Taylor than have to concern himself with Simon Rogers' unpredictable appearance. There was simply no need for Simon if Sam Taylor felt competent.

'OK – I'll head Simon off as long as you are confident that you can do the necessary. We will have to determine the insertion sequence and the interval between each image. I imagine that will simply be the programme length divided by four. The image sequence is not necessarily crucial because it's repeated – I suggest using it as it appears in Nigel Armstrong's message. That OK?'

Taylor nodded. 'No problem.'

'Oh, one thing more – the showing is supposed to be done with virgin copies. They know we augment our programmes and they don't want the showing to be with anything enhanced; not until it's broadcast. Please keep your doctored versions as "one offs" and then hand them to me for safe-keeping. Mark them "FT" with capitals – I'll explain later. Before that make two virgin copies of each programme and I will send them off for the BNU vetting. Just before the Westminster Hall screening we will exchange your versions for those they already have.'

'How the hell are you going to do that?'

'They have invited me to the showing – when I'm there I'll carry out the exchange… one way or another!'

It came as a shock – much more of a shock. On the morning he travelled to Westminster Hall he took the Underground instead of driving. The bus route was out of the question, too many service interruptions. At Temple, passenger numbers taking the Tube to various destinations were few, the trains were virtually empty, but the two stations he passed through were littered with the human wreckage that the BNU's policies had created. He'd seen many destitute families before in public places and on the streets, but now in the main railway and Underground stations they were crowded in, huddled in small encampments they had set up in corners and in the corridors between platforms. Most sat or lay on bedrolls, surrounded by whatever personal belongings they had managed to salvage from the houses and homes they had lost. Some had notices scrawled on sheets of cardboard asking for work, or appealing for money to stave off starvation. Some even offered their children for 'domestic service'. God alone knew what the consequences of that were. It was clear house evictions were still going on as the unemployment levels rose and the health and welfare budget was pruned to pay for the increased defence budget, extra police and the hated 'public warden' security forces.

When, at last, he sat in the District Line train looking up at the commercial posters pasted uppermost on the side of the carriage, he saw several that were familiar; they were the product of his own agency, the best that Morley, Swan & Bramly could provide.

It was ironic then that their effect was unlikely to justify the cost, time and effort that went into them. As matters stood, the current economic state was sufficiently dire to reduce the country's domestic economy to 70 per cent of what it had been. Too many were on the bread line to take notice of advertisements entreating them to purchase another brand of hair lacquer. He felt a pang of nostalgia for a time when everything seemed to move ahead rather than retreat backwards. As that emotion surfaced he also recalled how the current disaster had come about, and once again a surge of guilt filled him. He was even more resolved to carry out his mission. His only chance of redemption was contained in the three DVDs he carried in his inside coat pocket. He had left the agency offices that morning with a loving farewell from Margaret, who had acted as though he was going off to war. In a sense she had been right, he was at war – with his own conscience and his determination to rid the country of a blight.

On arrival at Westminster station he had walked quickly to the parliamentary estate and passed through the police cordons using his letter of invitation to the premiere showing of MS&B's ultimate tribute to the British National Union. He hoped never to have to repeat it.

Chapter 27

H<small>E WAS TOLD</small> that almost 1,200 people would have the privilege of viewing the three programmes his teams had produced, and to his surprise he could see from the neatly aligned rows of chairs that all 1,200 would be easily accommodated in the Great Hall. He was very early and the hall was virtually empty except for a small gaggle of ushers, menials and technicians gathered some distance away, their echoed conversation and occasional laughter reverberating around the walls.

He kept still, standing at the back of the vast space, surveying the hall's architecture and reminding himself of why he was there. As he looked above him at the superb hammer beam roof and the medieval eavesdroppers, it occurred to him that a quicker way of expediting the demise of so many government parasites would be for the roof to collapse. It would result in 176 tons of lead, a more than equal amount of buttressed masonry, and massive wooden beams, all falling inward and executing everyone present. However, as he felt the three DVDs in his inside pocket he dismissed the idle thought, given that the roof had remained intact for well over 600 years and was unlikely to have any political hostility.

At the front of the array of chairs was a huge semi-silver

screen and in the centre aisle, between the seats, a series of humped cable covers leading up to, and underneath, the screen. The covers he supposed were to defend the video cables leading to a colour projector behind the screen. Using a back projector was far simpler; it eliminated the need to hang a projector from the roof beams. The cables in turn led back between the chairs to a medium-sized booth at the back of the hall. It appeared to have been constructed to hold the video and DVD equipment and had been painted matt black. For all its new paint, he recognized it as a typical, but large, plastic garden outhouse. The side windows had been boarded up and he could see only one opening, a small porthole cut out at the front near the summit of the roof.

In the absence of any observation from the small number of bodies at the far end of the hall, he spotted a rear door and slipped in. He found himself contained in a darkened, somewhat claustrophobic cubicle, faintly lit by stray light entering from the small observation porthole at the front. This he assumed allowed sight of the screen some 45m away and was there to allow an operator to control the screen image.

In the dim light he made out a table with three DVD players and a video control unit for the projection equipment. Leading away from each DVD was a cluster of wires all routed to the control unit; they, in turn, had some thick cables leading down to the floor and disappearing under the front cubicle wall – therein were the video cables.

He powered up all three DVDs and pressed the various eject buttons. None presented a disk as the trays slid out, so he had to presume that the virgin versions of the DVDs were in the hands of whoever would be running the show.

It was very opportune, all he had to do was install the three modified DVDs and ensure that they were not replaced.

However, to do that he would have to intercept whoever it was bringing the virgin versions and controlling the viewing. For that he was obliged to wait – installing his versions too early might mean that they would then be replaced, and that would be a disaster.

He turned to leave the cubicle and at that moment the door opened and he impacted another body as it entered.

He instinctively turned to his side as a pair of hands, lifted in defence, pushed him away and made him stumble. He just managed to keep his feet and, as he turned back to face the incoming stranger a voice said, 'Christ – who are you?'

He was wholly unprepared for this direct physical encounter, particularly with the rather indistinct form in front of him, but he had previously rehearsed a response; a response intended to deflect any challenge regarding his presence in the cubicle.

'I might ask you the same question – and the answer had better be good.'

'I'm the only one authorized to be in here – I'm acting as the projectionist. I'm running the show. So who are you?'

'I didn't ask you what you were supposed to be doing here, I'm asking you who you are?'

He gave out an authoritative and intolerant tone, one that would brook no protest.

For a moment the other man remained silent.

Then he blurted 'Sod this,' turned on his heel, pushed open the door, and left.

It was not what he expected. He expected the man to argue his case, but not for him to abruptly quit the arena. He decided to give chase – he needed to persuade the man that he was not in possession of the right DVDs for the showing. Above all, he had to get the modulated DVDs screened.

Just as he was about to step out of the booth and onto the paved floor of the hall he heard voices. One became strident and he recognized the voice of the man he had just encountered. Another, calmer, voice he also recognized; was it Nicholas Frobisher, the BNU moneyman and now minister of finance?

He stepped out onto the hall floor to be met by a small group of men, one of whom, from his almost hysterical babble, was his earlier adversary. To the man's side was Nicholas Frobisher, presenting his usual sartorial elegance. Surrounding them were what seemed to be a few ministerial aids and bodyguards.

He stood his ground and waited.

Frobisher, his head still half turned to the complaining man then caught sight of him standing by the booth door.

'Good Lord – Elliot Mason, it's good to see you, Elliot. I had a feeling that our man here had mistaken the situation. He seems to think you were up to no good in the booth. I'm sure that wasn't the case. Is there a problem or were you just curious about how our technicians had arranged the equipment for the show?'

He was immensely relieved – Frobisher gave no sign of being suspicious. The man he had met in the booth was suddenly silenced and stood back sheepishly as Frobisher voiced his greeting.

'Hello Nicholas – I beg your pardon... good morning, Minister. Well, yes, you're right on both counts. I was in the booth to whet my curiosity and to talk to the individual handling the programme DVDs. There is a problem, which sadly we in MS&B created. We inadvertently failed to give full credit to everyone who helped compose the three programmes we are to see later on. Some of your political officers were not acknowledged in the list of credits so we had to remedy that, otherwise it would have been unfair. They worked very hard and should get the credit they deserve. I have the corrected DVDs with me, and intended to exchange the revised ones for the flawed ones I sent you. Simply a case of viewing one set rather than the other. Now Minister, may I have a private word?'

Frobisher looked puzzled but after a brief hesitation he nodded his head in agreement and stepped away from the throng around him. Then he walked around to the other side of the booth, instantly out of sight and the hearing of his entourage.

He followed on, a few steps behind Frobisher until he caught up.

'Now Elliot, if what you said just then is correct, you need say no more.'

'Not entirely. I wanted this said out of earshot of your retainers. My people made a mistake over the two sets of DVDs you wanted. The ones we sent you are enhanced. The ones here in my coat with "FT" marked on them are not. We used "FT" to identify each set – only the ones not enhanced have "FT" – the full title. The ones with the BNU political officers' names missing are enhanced. It is imperative that the two sets are exchanged otherwise the outcome will be catastrophic.'

For a moment Frobisher looked stunned, and then he smiled.

'I suppose these things happen, Elliot – it's a good thing you found out even if it is at the eleventh hour. What do you propose to do? Chaperone our man over there – make sure the right programmes are screened?'

He produced the three DVD cases.

'Yes, with me in attendance there's no chance of confusion – as I have pointed out, the corrected set has "FT" written on the case and the disk. "FT", as I've said, means "Full Title" – no enhancement, so I can't go wrong. As you suggest, I'll stay in the booth at the start of each programme and ensure all goes well.'

Frobisher gave a brief nod.

'I'll give the projectionist instructions to do as you say. Pity your seat at the front will be empty during the screening. I was going to introduce you to the PM, we might want your advice on a few things we've got in the pipeline. However, it can wait until after this morning's screening. All right Elliot, see you later.'

Chapter 28

'I'M SORRY MR ELLIOT, I was given definite instructions not to allow any one to tamper with the video equipment and when I saw you I...'

He gave a wide, but hardly visible smile to the man now in the cubicle with him, a man who was clearly anxious about keeping his job with the Ministry of Works. His name was Ralph Kepson and it seemed impossible to stop him narrating all his personal circumstances concerning his wife, children and his hard-pressed relatives. All the pain and adversity went back decades, and was blurted out at a surprisingly lucid rate. He'd disgorged most of his life's history by the time the FT disks had been placed in the replay DVD trays.

As far as he could determine, Kepson had become a willing ally only after he realized that Elliot Mason moved in exalted circles and could, in theory, make or break him. Kepson, apparently, saw the same state of affairs. He had no intention of countermanding anything Mr Mason wanted – to do so was tantamount to employment suicide.

And yet Kepson was a hindrance – with his close scrutiny there was always the risk that he would become a prime witness to what was about to happen.

'You can forget the earlier incident Ralph – I bear no grudges. You were only doing what you were told to do.

This procedure with the DVD playback is pretty simple; I've done it before. As soon as I have the first programme running, I'll set up the screen illumination so you can make yourself scarce and look for some coffee.'

It was a reasonable ploy but Kepson would only be gone for a short while and he was tempted to say, 'After that Ralph, why don't you watch the programmes? Tell me what you think – good or bad. An impartial opinion would be very valuable for future scripts.' If he complied, Kepson would go the way everyone else watching the programmes would go, and that would remove the only living witness.

As his suggestion about the coffee sank in, his unwanted companion said nothing at first and then, 'OK Mr Elliot, I'll see what I can do coffee-wise – you'll want one I imagine?'

'Sure, very white, two sugars please. Here, my treat.'

He handed Kepson a newly minted and BNU-designed five-pound note.

'Take your time – I'm not sure if the House refectory is open. See what you can do.'

Kepson grunted an acknowledgement and was soon gone.

Now he had to calculate his next move. He couldn't have Kepson around for too long – yet sure as hell the programme-watching suggestion was out of the question – he didn't want Kepson's wife and children to curse him for all eternity as the cold-blooded killer of a loving father; they didn't deserve it. No, on second thoughts this was one potentially fatal outcome he didn't want on his conscience.

As he wrestled with the problem, the solution suddenly occurred and it was fairly straightforward. It was opportune that the idea came to him when it did. The sounds of a large horde of people entering the hall and finding their seats came to him through the observation porthole in the booth. Chairs scraped on the flagstones and the babble of conversation ebbed and flowed.

It was almost time, and glad he was for it.

Ralph Kepson doubted that the coffee would still be palatable by the time he got back to the hall. It had taken a long time to find a coffee vending machine and to get the change to operate it. It would have been all the simpler if he had been allowed near the House refectory, but he'd been turned back as he tried to get in to the Palace of Westminster. Luckily he'd been directed to the vending machine below ground in the maintenance section but he'd been forced to wait until a lone worker turned up for refreshments and managed to change his five-pound note.

Now he was within a few yards of Westminster Hall with two rapidly cooling coffees, most of which had slopped onto the floors and staircases he'd had to negotiate.

Just as he came up to the small police cordon around the outside entrance, an armed policeman stepped forward.

'You Ralph Kepson?'

'Er, yes.'

'Message for you. Your wife's unwell. You've leave to go home and make sure everything is all right.'

'Oh Christ – my God when…?'

'Just now – come on, I'll escort you out.'

'These coffees – I need to deliver one.'

'Not necessary – stick them in the waste bin over there. No time to lose, come on.'

Kepson dumbly disposed of the coffees in the large bin to one side of the entrance. He then turned and followed the waiting policeman. At the entrance to the Great Hall Elliot Mason stepped into the sunlight and watched Kepson walk despondently away. Behind him, Mason could hear the sound track of the first BNU presentation. He never turned towards it, he wouldn't, not until he heard the last bars of music as the closing credits appeared and the audience showed its appreciation. Then it would be time for him to press 'play' on the second DVD player, leave the booth, and turn his back again.

He spent the days following the BNU screenings in apprehensive despair. He'd started to fear that the BNU assembly in the Great Hall had been unaffected by the programmes; there was no indication that the subliminal messages had made any difference. He even started to become short-tempered and claustrophobic as his ever-mounting anxiety caused the four walls of his office to close in on him.

There was no Margaret to calm him; he'd sent her away to her parents to avoid her seeing his joyous face as each announcement of a suicide came through. He had no wish to be seen as jubilant when the news broke – not when mass murder was involved.

But for an interminable time it didn't happen; there was no news in the media of anything catastrophic taking place around Westminster Palace.

All Margaret would have seen, had she been close, was a morose individual clearly on tenterhooks as inactivity and a brooding silence met all his scheming.

When Sam Taylor slipped into the office and asked in rather veiled terms how well the presentation had gone, he could only confirm that at first it had been problematic, but in terms of the showing, had met all expectations. Sam was pleased at the response and somewhat prophetic when on leaving the office he announced that 'it was now a case of fingers crossed and wait and see'. The 'wait and see' he spoke of was tantamount to torment.

Then one afternoon he heard the uproar, a flood of sound penetrating Margaret's office and seeping into his. As he opened the outer office door the work floor was in turmoil. He watched in amazement as people flew left and right, some with expressions of delight on their faces. He then saw Sam Taylor, his head poking above a set of partitions near the CGI section. He too seemed thrilled about something. He made his way forward, and as he came within shouting distance of Sam Taylor he heard someone blurt out 'Feldt's gone – he's dead, so are lots of the others.'

As the news came to him it was as if a huge load had been lifted from his shoulders. He was no longer tortured by his deeds. His anguish was, for the moment, extinguished. Not even his previous deep sense of guilt languished anywhere in his soul – he was free.

Chapter 29

WHILE THE DESTRUCTION of the government was ongoing it seemed to him that the centre of London was far from the safest place to be. Word came to his staff by telephone and text that suicide had eliminated scores of government officials and this fact was rapidly disseminated through the bush telegraph. The media too had reported the inexplicable deaths of scores of BNU party members, including most of the top-ranking ministers. It was reported that some had found a railway line, laid across the rails and been decapitated, others simply drove cars at high speed into concrete walls. Yet others had overdosed on prescription medicine. The River Thames, so the reports went, had numerous drowned bodies all floating towards the sea. A few simply climbed to the walkways around the roofline of the Houses of Parliament and threw themselves off.

The horrific ends of a good few were witnessed by bystanders, many of whom were still loyal to the BNU. Very soon, as it became clear what was happening, crowds began to protest against 'recidivist murderers' and 'anti-democratic enemies of the state' while those inherently hostile to the administration took the end of a detested government as a divine blessing. The result was a slow but ever-increasing rise of mob warfare that only took a few hours to evolve.

He decided to send everyone home, but as the day progressed the idea became less and less sensible and pragmatic. Fleet Street started to look and sound like a war zone as the population of London and the police force itself began to fragment into political factions. Some of his staff, who had ventured down into the underground car park, returned quickly to report that on the street, some way off, they could see armed riot police fighting mobs made up of civilians, public wardens, other armed police and even young teenagers. It wasn't hard to believe – even with their offices in an elevated position, the sound and the fury was evident.

He called Sam Taylor into his office and locked the outer and inner doors. Taylor took a desk-side seat. He sat with restless and fidgeting fingers, clearly agitated by the situation.

'Bloody mess, Elliot – never could have envisaged this happening. A few of our staff, apparently still imprinted from the BNU electoral campaign, are making waves. Those free of it can keep the others calm but if things get out of hand I really don't know what to suggest. I'm sorry I haven't been with you lately – I've had a lot to contend with. How do you feel now that most of the BNU hierarchy appear to have succumbed to the imprinting?'

'If you must know, bloody glad. We did what we set out to do and that was to right a wrong. It worked; it had to, so damn the consequences. I've absolutely no regrets, nor should you.'

Taylor shook his head. 'I can't explain it, but it hit me harder than I expected. I'm no less culpable than you, and I hated the bloody BNU, so I should feel as you do... and yet...'

'Sam, forget it. It's over. Would you feel better if we could reverse what has just happened? I don't think so.'

'I suppose not, Elliot – what's next?'

'Well, I don't think this insurrection can go on indefinitely – sooner or later I assume the pro-BNU lot will decondition and come to their senses just as our own people will. However, in the meantime we must take care of all our people. I believe we will have to wait for some while before things settle down, so if we do have to use our offices as a safe haven tonight we should think about how long it might take. Do we have food?'

'Don't know, Elliot, I'll check the canteen and see what's in store. If we can feed everyone tonight and maybe contrive a small breakfast in the morning, we may find that tomorrow is a bit less traumatic out on the streets and we can start to get staff out of here.'

He gave a reassuring nod of his head. 'All right, Sam, that's a reasonable objective, but what about the other levels in this block – I mean all the other firms from the ground floor up? What are they doing staff-wise? Have any vacated?'

Taylor shook his head vigorously. 'Not as far as I know – they'd be daft to risk travelling when things are as bad as they are at the moment. The problem is we are the only outfit in this block with a partially stocked canteen. As far as I know the rest depend on what are… were… the local sandwich bars, cafés and pubs. If they are trapped in this building like us they are going to have a very uncomfortable night. If you want me to, I'll reconnoitre the other floors and see what's going on.'

He gave a faint shake of his head. 'No, I don't think that would be a good idea – I hate to say it but this is a case of us having to be selfish. I don't want you to attract their attention and have us invaded by hungry members of other firms. Leave well enough alone, Sam. Now—'

Suddenly all the lights were extinguished and apart

from the distant street noise, everything reverted to a tense hush.

Sam Taylor gave him a grim look. 'Christ, the grid's probably gone down, looks like some power stations have been shut down or the fighting has wrecked the local sub-stations. There are no stand-by generators in this block so we are stymied.'

They both stood, not sure of what needed to be done.

'Look, Sam – take some of our boys with you and pop down to the underground electrics cabin by the car park and see if anything on the electrical distribution side has tripped. If not get yourselves back up here immediately. And while you are at—'

To his amazement the telephone rang – the first time since the presentation in the Great Hall.

He flicked his head at Taylor to get him on his way and then picked up the phone.

'Elliot Mason.'

Without any polite introduction a voice he recognized came on – only this time it was a hostile and very menacing Nicholas Frobisher.

'You unspeakable bastard, Mason – I had my suspicions when we met in Westminster Hall that you were playing a double game, and it's a damn good thing I let those suspicions deflect me from watching those fucking malicious programmes of yours. You've effectively destroyed this country's executive... but not all of it; I'm still here, and as the last senior minister I have assumed full administrative control. As soon as I have called in the army to crush the uprisings, and I have regained public order, I will have you arrested and shot as a mass murderer; it's far better than you deserve. Almost sixteen state funerals will take place because of you and that is far from the end of it. You are a bloody traitor – we gave you our trust and you repaid it with treachery. Watch out Mason, I will settle with you soon.'

For a brief second he felt helpless and then a rising resentment lifted his nerve.

'You degenerate shit, Frobisher. Pity you aren't included in the death toll – but that's an oversight which I intend to correct as soon as I can. If you think I'm going to sit still, have you blame me for this mess and wait for your assassins to come after me you are mistaken. Instead of issuing warnings in my direction why don't you start watching your back? There are a good many who would rejoice over seeing you dead – not only me. You think you can assume power on your own – think again.'

'I have thought, and I have taken power, by replacing the prime minister, so you can eat your words. Watch out, Mason, I'm coming after you.'

As Frobisher's last words were uttered, the line went dead.

He just listened, his audacity terminated and with his spine frozen by foreboding.

What to do now?

Words were all very well, but what was clear to him was that if he was to stay alive he had to get to Frobisher, before Frobisher got to him.

As his hand let go of the phone, gently replacing it back in its cradle with unnecessary care, Sam Taylor pushed back the office door and hastened in. As Taylor closed the door behind him he saw Elliot Mason leaning over the desk phone with his head cowed forward.

'Trouble?'

'Yeah, and then some. We didn't get them all; Frobisher is still alive and attempting to recover control. That was him on the phone – promising me a very swift death.'

Taylor snorted with disgust.

'Some hopes – he and his thugs would have to get at you

here, and with the unrest on the streets I can't see it happening. No! For the moment I think you're safe.'

'Perhaps, but I can't rely on it – I have to get to Frobisher and what's left of the BNU before they get to me. Sam, are there any TV channels still transmitting?'

'I think so – a lot of the commercial entertainment channels went off the air earlier, but one or two of the news channels are still transmitting. BBC's OK, so are most of the US-based channels but I imagine there is still some more UK coverage here and there. Why do you ask?'

'I ask because I want to transmit a message, on every screen still switched on. I want a message that will prevent anyone watching from joining anything Frobisher and his surviving cronies want done.'

Taylor's face suddenly lit with understanding.

'A subliminal, yes? Something like "Don't obey any government edict or order". Is that what you're thinking of?'

'I am... can you do it?'

Taylor nodded vigorously but then looked worried.

'Of course, were we operating normally, but the problem is two-fold. First, getting any programme to the TV studios. They would have to be London-based for quickness, CNN, BBC National, BBC World News, European... any in fact we can get at. I suppose we might be able to email it, but it's doubtful, the file content limit would apply. Second, without power – and, by the by, it's nothing to do with the power house down below – we can't use the video editing desk, so whatever we might do otherwise, we're thwarted.'

'Yeah, damn... let's hope we get power back in time. OK Sam, see what you can do. Incidentally, the message you just concocted earlier is ideal, use it if the opportunity arises. Now, what about tonight – food?'

'Oh yeah – good news. We cook by gas and I believe we have enough to feed everyone for tonight with unlimited tea and coffee throughout. Likewise tomorrow – a small breakfast can be arranged. It won't be very big, but enough.'

'OK, thanks Sam, and as far as the subliminal message is concerned the sooner you can get to it the better; and I suggest a touch more delta.'

He watched as Taylor lifted a hand in acknowledgement and departed. If power was restored, all that needed to be done was to get the subliminal messages to the TV studios – if it was at all possible.

Chapter 30

H<small>E WAS TEMPTED</small>, very tempted to make a break for it. To not be where Frobisher believed he was.

Being in his office, or out on the agency floor, exacerbated his sense of being trapped. And he knew he would not be relieved of the feeling until he had negated the threat from Frobisher; or whoever it was Frobisher was sending to carry out his deadly intentions.

He found he could temporarily silence his own misgivings by moving around the various agency teams, trying to encourage them to keep their projects going and thus divert any chance of a tinderbox reaction. Like him, he knew they were all developing a siege mentality. All he needed was for one member of staff to panic, and regardless of the risk on the streets, there could be a tidal wave of people trying to get away. It wasn't just his concern for the individuals themselves; he recognized, somewhat selfishly, that a desperate escape would be synonymous with the end of Morley, Swan & Bramly. If people died it was unlikely he could replicate the same quality of personnel he had at present.

Some way into the afternoon he smelled food being cooked in the cafeteria and was reassured as he heard staff begin to comment on how appetizing the aroma was, and that they were looking forward to a meal. As some of the teams started to migrate towards the cafeteria the overhead fluorescent lights flashed on, died for a second, and then came on permanently. As they did so there were cheers and expressions of relief. To him, however, it meant far more. He turned and saw Sam Taylor heading towards the video-editing desk. It was timely – the plan could still work.

The CGI staff were huddled around another screen but it was hard to discern what it was they were looking at. Suddenly they broke apart with a sudden outpouring of disgust. He could see that they had been watching a TV channel, and on screen was a stone-faced man he knew well – it was Frobisher.

One of the CGI people turned to address the rest of the floor.

'The bastard is calling for calm – says he's ordering out the police and army and will impose a daytime curfew for three days. No one is to be seen on the streets on pain of arrest. Looters are to face execution. Apparently, the assassination of the government leaders was planned by a few rabid revolutionary factions; so too the current insurrection. The few traitors involved will be summarily dealt with, he says. He wants all police and public wardens to take their posts and suppress the unrest until the army can mobilize. The disingenuous shit – he finished by saying he depends on the loyalty of the populace and those who believe in the aims of the Party. Wants everyone to remember that their duty is to national recovery and a return to stable government.'

'Well I know what government I want us to return to,' a voice shouted, 'and it ain't the one Frobisher wants.'

There were cheers and a general chorus of agreements.

He smiled to himself – his people were definitely on the change.

As the clock neared 5.30 p.m., he watched many more staff wander towards the cafeteria, and as he neared it he could see a high percentage of tables already occupied and laden with well-filled plates of food.

However, it was not his stomach that engaged his mind – it was the fact that he could not discount Frobisher's threat. He knew that eventually the street fighting would die down enough for general movement, and that he would be a sitting duck the moment Frobisher's paid thugs realized they could get through.

There was no doubt about it; it was time to go.

As his mind attempted to work out what would be involved in an escape plan, he began to think about Margaret – now safely ensconced with her parents. What troubled him was the fact that he had not heard from her. Every couple of days he expected a phone call from her parents' house, but now it was becoming too long an interval since he last spoke to her.

He decided to make contact if he could and returned to his office. Once he knew she was well, he resolved to ignore previous assurances and put distance between himself and the agency. The latter as soon as he had thought of a secure passage.

He knew her number by heart and stood by his desk as he dialled. As his fingers punched the keyboard he was able to look out of his window to the street below and noted that the law courts were still smoking. The recent fighting had left many of the other buildings scarred and disfigured, with shattered windows and the walls pockmarked by small arms fire. Here and there, hunched against a wall or face down on the pavement, he could see the abandoned dead. A few in police uniforms were stretched out like blue-coloured blotches on the road. Except for these chilling examples he could see nothing else to indicate any dangerous activity. It looked as though the area was now deserted. With the day coming to an end, if ever there was an appropriate time to go, this was it.

Again, as he scanned both sides of the street it confirmed his first assessment; the short, but ferocious, battles had moved on. All that denoted the earlier insurrections and lawlessness were the skyward plumes of blue-black smoke with flame-tinted fringes and funnels of red-hot embers lifting off the far-away horizon. But they were sufficiently distant to offer him hope – he might yet get through.

He tried Margaret's number but to no avail. It rang and rang until the ring tone cut off as the time limit came in. He tried again, with exactly the same result. Once again he scanned the outside – it still appeared to be peaceful. If he was to leave it had to be now.

He grabbed his coat and car keys and made for the outer office. Just at that moment Sam Taylor pushed through the anteroom door. Realizing what was about to happen, he stared at him in horror.

'Oh! Christ, Elliot – are you going to try to make for home? If so, can I let everyone else go? It seems a lot safer now; I'm tempted myself.'

'Yeah Sam, I'm on my way out, but not to get home. I've some unfinished business with someone.'

Taylor gave him an inquisitive look.

'Don't tell me you're going after Frobisher – how on earth do you think you can track him down? It's an odds-on bet he'll be guarded... bloody public wardens no doubt. You'll never get near him.'

'You may be right, on my own it's not going to be easy. If I had some help it would be another matter.'

'What do you mean – a compatriot, an accomplice?'

'Yes, just that. I have to draw Frobisher out into the open.

There are two rifles on the road out there. If I can get hold of a rifle and get close enough, I'm pretty sure I can nail him. What I need is for someone to take his interest and get him to stand still for thirty seconds – that's all.'

'Bloody hell Elliot, "that's all" you say? You have no idea where he is at the moment. You could come up against an impossible situation.'

'I'm fairly sure I know where he is at the moment – either Number Ten or Number Eleven Downing Street. He wouldn't miss the chance of having access to the prime minister's residence. I'd lay odds that he's there.'

Taylor rubbed his chin and then gripped his nose between thumb and forefinger. He said nothing, as he looked inward at his own reservations.

'Look Elliot, the message we wanted broadcast has gone to every station still operating. You may not need to...'

'Yes I will – with Frobisher still exercising control we can't be sure of the outcome. Better my way.'

Again he had to wait as Taylor pondered his options.

'You any good with a rifle, Elliot? Ever fired one in anger?'

'No. What about you?'

'Better than you, Elliot. My father taught me when I was a youth, he was ex-army and his hobby was competition shooting. He shot at Bisley and other ranges. I suggest that you be the bait and I'll be the sniper – I won't miss.'

There was no contest. If Sam was volunteering and confident he could do it, who was he to argue?

'OK Sam, good. I've changed my mind by the way. Anyone else wanting to risk it can go too – it's up to them, but they must follow us out. I don't want our departure blocked.'

'I'll spread the word, Elliot. If you're ready I'll get my things.'

'Just one thing, Sam – what about the basement car park? Can we get out?'

Taylor turned. 'When I was down there earlier the security barriers were still closed. All we have to do is override the safety interlocks and we're out. So too everyone else.'

'Great, we go first, pick up the weapons and scoot.'

'OK, fingers crossed.'

Chapter 31

THE UNDERGROUND CAR park was dark and deserted. Apart from a few flourescent strips the car park was mainly illuminated by fingers of daylight bleeding in through the heavy steel grills of the security gates.

A slight incline, a ramp, led cars up and down to street level on a twin tarmac access. Each had its own barrier, beyond which were the security gates – both of which had been locked down like a portcullis. Apart from the front security doors, used as a public and staff entrance, the underground car park gates were the only other way in and had ensured the office block could not be easily invaded. These gates were strong, built to withstand any assault other than with anti-tank artillery.

He stood on the 'out' ramp, looking up through the gates at street level as Sam Taylor made for the car park security booth. The booth contained the switching gear for the security gates and had to work if they were to break out.

'I'm ready, Elliot – OK out there?'

'I think so... no movement close to us, but then, I can't see too far.'

'We'll have to chance it. Here goes.'

He waited for what seemed a never-ending time before he heard a deep hum and the electric motors kicked in. As they did so, the barriers started to lift. With just enough room to duck under the barriers as they rose, he scrambled out of the entrance and slowly made his way up to the street. He ignored the concrete dust and road dirt that now soiled his suit – now was not the time for sartorial concerns. He knew it was dangerous coming out onto the street but there was little choice; he had to expose himself to any waiting sniper if he was to get at the weapons they needed. He crouched on the pavement, looking right and left at the strange conditions around him. A cold, uncanny silence gripped the area, only interrupted by a slight, far-off noise akin to a distant train. It all seemed utterly deserted and except for the bodies lying across the road, there was no human presence anywhere.

It was unsettling and it instilled a tangible reluctance in him not to move or disturb anything. It was only as he felt the arrival of Sam Taylor behind him that he knew he was committed, and there was no turning back.

'OK Elliot, see anything threatening?'

'No – still nothing.'

'Where are the weapons? Ah, I see one.'

'On the far side there?'

'Yeah, I'll go for it.'

'There's another two on this side. I'll take them.'

'Ready to break?'

'Ready when you are, Elliot. My car engine is running, the moment we've got the rifles, and we get back here, we scoot.'

'OK – go!'

Running across to the body lying on the opposite pavement seemed to take an age. Fleet Street had width, but to him it seemed wider than the Grand Canyon. Every lurching step promised the fateful shot, ending ignominiously everything he had planned and was intent on doing. He felt an inward shiver and wondered what it was like to be hit by a bullet – particularly one that didn't kill you immediately. Was it excruciating pain and then an agonizing transition into oblivion? Nearing the blue-uniformed body, he still hoped he wasn't going to find out.

He'd been a big man, but the pool of congealed blood that had leaked from his head testified to the fact that a bullet through the head killed you whatever size you were.

He bent down over the prostrate form, grabbed the assault rifle and pulled up. The hand wrapped around the trigger grip and the arm attached to it came up too, and he found himself struggling with inflexible rigor mortis. To his dismay the weapon would not separate from the hand and he began to think about abandoning the quest. In desperation he stood up, clamped the arm to the ground with his foot and then twisted the rifle away from the grip. With one supreme effort he tore it towards him and as he gained possession, was almost instantly dashing back the way he had come.

For a fleeting second he looked up at his office block and was amazed to see faces on every level staring out of the windows at him. Were they collectively wishing him a safe return or, as in the Roman arena, wishing for blood? Maybe they saw him as a pathfinder – someone lacking in fear. If so, he certainly hoped he could find the courage they expected of him.

Nearing the entrance he saw the nose of a black Ford sitting on the 'out' ramp with Sam Taylor in the driver's seat. The boot lid and passenger door were open and he assumed Sam had the boot open for storing the weapons.

Almost losing his footing as he rounded the rear of the car, he recovered and dropped the rifle into the boot next to two others. He slammed the lid down, leapt forward and threw himself into the passenger seat, pulling the door shut as he felt the seat wrap around him. Without a pause Sam

Taylor punched down the accelerator and the car surged forward.

The exit was too fast and as Taylor pulled the car around for a tight turn it felt as though the car would roll. It righted itself with a sudden lift of the suspension and Taylor gunned the car down towards the ravaged law courts. There was nothing in the way of traffic or people to stop them and as they passed the gaunt and smoking law courts and neighbouring buildings, it drove home just how much damage had been done. And yet there was no human presence; as they drove, hardly a person was visible.

'Where are we going, Sam? Are you taking the Embankment?'

'Yes, but we aren't heading directly towards Downing Street – if you want Frobisher my guess is that getting into Downing Street the front way will be virtually impossible. I'm heading towards Horse Guards Parade, then to the back of the parade ground. If I remember correctly Downing Street gardens back on to Horse Guards. There's a big wall separating the gardens from Horse Guards, which we will have to scale after we're certain the rear of Number Ten isn't guarded. As I once found, when we get to the Mountbatten memorial we cut through two tree lines and then we're at the back of Number Ten. After that we need sight of Frobisher before we can do anything – it may be a long wait.'

He nodded his agreement and kept his eyes on the road as Taylor sped through the streets. Now and then he saw movement – small gaggles of people who quickly disappeared into doorways, hurried away or turned their backs as they drove past. For all the people living and working in London it was as though a great plague had wiped out almost the entire population. At least he didn't get sight of any police, army, armed wardens or vigilantes as they approached Horse Guards – he hoped it would stay like that.

He now felt a sense of release.

'You OK Elliot – still sure?'

'Yes, and I feel a bit more confident. Having the weapons helps, if Frobisher's thugs try to intercept us we can at least fight back.'

Taylor gave a wan grin. 'I might, but you'd probably send your rounds in my direction. But don't worry, we'll remedy that.'

To their surprise the security guards at the parade ground had fled their posts, leaving the entrance unmanned and open. It was only a few moments drive for them to reach the Mountbatten memorial, retrieve their weapons and abandon the car.

The rear garden wall of Number Ten was high and offered no easy way of scaling it. However, it was just possible to see the upper floors of the prime minister's residence so long as they were far enough back. Laying down by the memorial made it possible to see a reasonably wide view of the rear and gave a good line of sight for a shot. But it was not good enough.

'We have to get into the garden,' he conceded. 'If he stays on the ground floor or isn't near a window we'll never get him.'

'Stay there, Elliot, I'm going back to the car. I think I have a towrope in the boot. We'll scale the wall with it.'

In a brooding silence, only interrupted by a breeze filtering through the trees, he waited in anticipation as Taylor scurried away. He looked down at the three rifles beside him, not knowing what to do with any of them. Even if Frobisher suddenly appeared a yard in front of him, he would be utterly useless.

He picked one up and tried to aim it. It was heavier than he expected and he felt nervous about handling it. The grip handle made it easier to pull the butt into his shoulder and his left hand seemed to automatically slip around the furniture surrounding the barrel, but he kept his finger back from the trigger, unsure if the weapon was still loaded and ready to fire.

As he held the rifle he became less apprehensive about using it and hoped that Sam Taylor would return quickly to give him the basics of marksmanship. He really didn't want Taylor to do his dirty work; if anyone was going to eliminate Frobisher it should be him. But so far Taylor was conspicuous by his absence – where the hell was he?

As the thought came, he heard the sound of a car engine some distance away. Surely Sam wasn't moving the car, and if he was, for what reason?

It was another few minutes before he heard movement behind him and Sam Taylor appeared through the trees.

'Where's the rope?'

'I didn't get it – there's an executive car just driven onto the parade ground back there and it's parked. I have a feeling that it's waiting for something or someone. Like to make a bet it's a small plane or helicopter?'

He gave an inward sigh of relief. Who would have commandeered a helicopter other than the temporary premier of the country? It had to be Frobisher, and soon to be out in the open if he was arriving by air. Better than attempting an impossible shot at Number Ten.

'I can't hear any aircraft at the moment... we may have a little time, Sam. Listen, show me how to use one of these rifles, I can't let you take all the responsibility if Frobisher turns up.'

Taylor looked unsure but then nodded his head.

'Pick up that one and let's see you aim it.'

He did as he had before, pulling the rifle into his shoulder and looking down over the open sights.

'Good – maybe you're a natural. OK, your rifle is unlikely

to need an exchange of magazines; they were nearly all full when I checked them so you have damn near twenty-eight rounds. I hope we won't get into a long drawn-out fire fight, so all you need to do is deselect safety... this one here... and you are ready to fire either fully automatic or single shot. At the moment I have selected single shot. For God's sake don't switch to fully automatic – unless you are used to the way the weapon behaves your rounds will go everywhere. Now, fore sight covers target and aligns with back sight, you take breath, hold it, and then squeeze the trigger. Expect some recoil. Understood?'

'Yes I do. Now, let's get back to where you saw the other car and pray they don't see ours.'

Taylor shook his head. 'They won't, I moved it – that is, I pushed it further behind those trees in front of the monument, that's why I was late back. If they see it they'll think it's abandoned. The best vantage point is between the same trees, we can stay hidden there and overlook the parade ground.'

He picked up the rifle and waited while Taylor did the same with the remaining two.

They turned and made for the first tree line, only stopping when the growth between two trees was dense enough for camouflage.

It was almost ideal – the parade ground stretched out in front of them and the parked car was clearly visible. It was a large Jaguar XF2 and notable as one used by the government hierarchy. Two men dressed in suits stood by it, and both appeared to be carrying automatic weapons.

'Still can't hear anything,' Taylor whispered. 'I hope to God it arrives soon... whatever it is.'

'Can't be a conventional aircraft Sam, the parade ground isn't long enough for a winged aircraft to land.'

Just then he heard it, as did Taylor.

'Chopper – coming in. Get ready. Hit the chopper first, fuel tank if you can.'

They hung on as the sound steadily increased and the helicopter suddenly burst into view, coming in low with a thunderous reverberating and rotor beating cacophony of sound. It hovered for a short time and then dropped down to land no more than 30m away. The whine of the turbo prop began to die down almost immediately, and as the rotor blades began to slow, the side door of the machine opened and a short set of steps folded on to the ground. Almost immediately an armed man stepped out, followed by another. They stood by, waiting for a third man to exit the helicopter. As the third body came out and his feet made contact with the top step, Taylor said 'Fire!'

It came as a shock. As Mason turned to his right Sam Taylor was lying prostrate, his legs slightly apart and his upper body wrapped around a rifle. Mason was already aiming and, as his eyes took in what Taylor was doing, his ears exploded as the first round was fired. He was slightly forward so his ear was closer to the muzzle. The sound was so explosive, so loud, that his ears immediately rang and then reverted to a high-pitched whistle. Even before Mason could react to what he had been told to do, Taylor fired again.

Half deaf and dazed, Mason was still able to realize that he had to get to work – he had to back Taylor up and ensure that they were successful.

He pulled the rifle into his shoulder and peered down the sights. The targets were obvious although there was now only one man visibly still alive. One body, prostrate on the ground, indicated the fate of the second guard and the accuracy of Taylor's marksmanship. The third and fourth had vanished back into the helicopter.

'Get the helicopter, Elliot, the other bastard is firing back and I'll have to deal with him. Don't fuck about!'

He shifted his sighting until it covered the rear of the helicopter and then squeezed the trigger.

The kick was unexpected, the blast deafening. With his ears still ringing he locked down his position and kept firing, seeing the cartridge cases eject sideways. He counted his rounds, now wondering if Taylor's assertion that he would not need more than twenty-eight rounds was to be tested.

He let go another four rounds but began to feel his shooting was poor – it had no discernible effect. He aimed again, freezing any tremor in the sights by tightening his grip on the rifle to the maximum.

As his fifth round raced towards its target there came a muffled explosion and the helicopter erupted in a giant ball of fire. Within seconds it was entirely swallowed by flames, all reaching out to swiftly engulf the car and the last living bodyguard. Their heads instinctively dropped forward into the grass to shield their faces. Then, as the seconds passed and the heat and shockwave dissipated, they both slowly came upright at the same time, looking at the two blazing vehicles and the ever-widening spiral of smoke and red-hot embers. Astonished and mesmerized by the spectacle, they stayed silent. It was hard to believe that their own hands had caused it. As the inferno thrived and blossomed, and the heat radiated further out, they were forced to withdraw behind foliage in the tree line. Taylor, still shielding his face with his hand, shook his head slowly.

'You reckon Frobisher was definitely in it, Elliot?'

'Yes. I got a glimpse of the man about to exit the helicopter – it was Frobisher all right. I don't think he survived, do you?'

Taylor smiled an ironic but regretful smile.

'No – somehow I don't think he did, and perhaps that ends it. If it's all over, Elliot, what are you going to do, any plans?'

'Well, I know where Margaret is at the moment and I think I would like to see her again, say within the next twenty-four hours if possible. I'm not convinced I'll live to tell the tale any longer if the remnants of Frobisher's assassination crew are still following orders. The sooner I'm on my way the better.'

Taylor scowled. 'No way, Elliot – you're too pessimistic, anything or anyone Frobisher and the BNU have left behind will be digging deep foxholes and escaping the fall out. I can't believe you have anything to fear.'

He listened to Sam Taylor's emphatic declaration with misgivings. And yet he wanted Sam's opinion to be right – to have the optimistic insight he did not. As he spoke, Taylor stood in a fixed stance, holding his rifle across his chest and posing as though modelling for a war memorial. It was strangely appropriate. For Taylor the battle was over and he had nothing but confidence for the future. He hoped some more of it would rub off onto him. He collected his thoughts: he wanted to see Margaret, even if, worst case, it might be for only a short time.

'Sam, could you drive me back to the agency so I can collect my car?'

'Sure – no problem.'

'What about you, Sam, what do you plan to do?'

'Me? I'm just hoping for a return to normality – eventually back to work like you I suppose.'

He shook his head.

'No... not like me, Sam. I've had it. I don't care if I never get to see another TV commercial, animation or poster under development. What I've done, what we've been through, I never want to repeat. If I never hear the word "subliminal" again I don't think I will ever be sorry. I've seen the light and now that my conscience is clear I'm tempted to change my life – perhaps I'll go into politics if I survive. Yes, I'd like to think I'll stand as a prospective Member of Parliament at the next general election... wherever and whenever that comes about. You might even vote for me, Sam, who knows? If you do, I will forever be grateful, but not as grateful as I am now for your loyalty, friendship and bravery. I can't tell you how I appreciate what you have done for me – you will always be welcome in my house.'

Taylor bowed his head in pleasurable embarrassment.

'Well, thanks for that, Elliot, and I empathize with your view. May I say that on the latter I reciprocate; and I'm really sorry to hear you've decided to forego returning to the agency. The boys and girls will miss you. Your predecessor was outstanding, but not a touch on you. You were the best boss we've ever had. But on reflection, what I did wasn't all for you. Remember, I was part of your plot with the BNU – before and after. I had my own deep misgivings; my own scruples got rubbed up the wrong way too. What we did today has evened the score... for both of us. I hope you agree. Come on, I think its time to get you to Margaret, the sooner the better I think.'

Chapter 32

As Sam Taylor took the wheel of their car to begin the return journey to Fleet Street and the agency, a feeling of apprehension descended on Mason again. To assume that with the demise of Frobisher the fascist autocracy was at an end could be over-optimistic and premature. Were all the BNU elite dead? It would only take a few second- or third-level party toadies to organize a replacement administration and the battle would be on again. He was utterly averse to the idea that he might stay on and cross swords with the BNU once more – he no longer had the nerve or the brazen bravado that had carried him through the recent BNU encounters. He'd been driven by a desire to make amends, but now it was done and enough was enough.

As the car negotiated its way through the relatively short distance to their base, it was through an atmosphere of progression – as though a new dawn had occurred. Mason was resolute in the direction he wanted to take; what he had told Sam Taylor was irreversible, he was going to wash his hands of his previous and current life. If indeed his and Sam's actions on the parade ground had effectively killed off the vestiges of government, and they had brought an end to the festering sore that afflicted the country, and if they had made it possible to replace it with something far more civilized, then amen, and he would sleep more peacefully. If not, it was for others to undermine the evil. There were others out there equally determined, he knew.

With his life no longer plagued by a sense of guilt, evident ever since he had soiled his hands with the BNU gold, Mason was now presented with the final question – would he surrender the money he had taken?

He no longer had any doubts. No he wouldn't!

He had been absolved of his past crimes. He had no need of any more contrition, repentance or remorse. What he and Sam had done had atoned for all the wrongs, and if he survived the next few months then he was never going to feel bad about it again.

As he pondered on his options, Sam Taylor said nothing. They travelled through roads and streets almost as deserted as when they had driven to the parade ground. It was only as they negotiated the access to Fleet Street that they began to notice more people spilling out into the open air. Then a few cars came towards them, one even blowing its horn.

Taylor suddenly turned to him.

'Christ, Elliot, I wonder – has the message got through? You know, the one I composed before we left, the "Don't obey any government edict or order". It could be that every-one is responding to it. Dear God, I hope so.'

They had their answer very soon as more and more bodies came out of offices, shops and buildings. Some waved, others just appeared to stand stock-still and suck in fresh air. Yet others joined hands and walked along pavements; a few simply hung out of windows calling out to those below.

By the time Taylor stopped the car outside their offices a few small crowds had formed, some of them made up of faces they knew from their own staff. It appeared that not all had had the courage to follow Elliot and Sam Taylor when they left. But now the elated faces gave credence to one thing

– now it was safe, the people had decided that come what may, the dictatorship was over. Whatever the machinations of a few diehards, the BNU would never be re-instated. Like its executive, it had expired.

Epilogue

This article by Dr Robert Chalmers was first published in *History Today* magazine in November 2058 and constitutes perhaps the most condensed yet factual comment on what is now called the 'Fascist Interval' in British government.

IN MEMORIUM – ELLIOT MASON AND THE SUBLIMINAL ENIGMA

Robert Chalmers

The death was announced on 20 September 2058 of Sir Elliot Mason MP, made famous as the man that instigated, and then destroyed, the short-lived dictatorship of the British National Union. He was widely thought to have perfected the use of subliminal imprinting (SI) in controlling human decision-making by employing quasi hypnotic imprinting through human delta wave modulation of a picture's luminance. It was this technique that supposedly underpinned the reasons he was able to indoctrinate the electorate into voting an overwhelming mandate for the former British National Union in the 2025 general election. (The BNU was banned in 2032 and is now illegal as a subversive and anti-democratic organisation.)

It is however, like many of the stories surrounding Mason, a myth.

Contrary to what has been spread by rumour and hearsay, Mason did not 'invent' subliminal imprinting nor did he exploit it entirely for his own personal gain. His role in the story is far more incidental to the supposed science and application of SI than is believed, although without his trust in its efficacy, and its overriding worth, the history of the UK would have been radically different.

Mason was born in 1982 in the village of Wyle in Wiltshire. Both of his parents were local to the village: his father a farm manager and his mother a county councillor. Both were politically active.

Mason, an MA in history and politics from Oxford, had stumbled into the world of commercial advertizing when, as a young graduate, he took a job as an advisor to a parliamentary candidate's campaign. His 'visionary' management regarding the promotion posters resulted in him being offered a permanent (though junior) position with the advertising agency handling the political campaign. Thereafter, and for a short time working with Jonathan Woodbridge (the person he would later succeed at the advertising agency of Morley, Swan & Bramly) he rose through the ranks.

Now that the one surviving member of the team that helped him employ subliminal imprinting has at last published his recollections of his engagement with Mason (*Armstrong N. Mason and Me*, Butterworth, 2056) we are able to piece together the complete series of incidents and episodes that led to Mason establishing his incredible place in British political history.

It appears from the interviews given by Sir Elliot's wife Margaret (neé Delaney, who survives him) that the rumours that Mason was not the first to use SI are true. According to her Jonathan Woodbridge, Mason's predecessor as CEO at

Morley, Swan & Bramly, had already used SI as an experiment in the Autoclean car wash commercial (2023/4) with outstanding results. The initiative for this came from Dr Emma Lilton and Mr Mike Crossly, both ex-employees of the now defunct Longmore Research Establishment located near Ashdown, Kent. Apparently Lilton and Crossly had carried out covert SI research programmes while employed at Longmore and, when made redundant and seeking employment, had approached Jonathan Woodbridge with their results. Impressed by the experimental results, and facing growing criticism over his business handling of MS&B, Woodbridge agreed to test the SI effect on one of his forthcoming TV commercials. The phenomenal Autoclean success justified the decision to employ SI and it was intended to use it again. However, all three behind the process were subsequently killed in a road accident on the day the Autoclean sales results were published. The Autoclean commercial and its success became iconic within the advertising world.

Subsequent to this tragedy, Elliot Mason was rapidly appointed as Woodbridge's successor and according to his wife (then his secretary) almost immediately made enquiries about the method underlining the Autoclean success. It was only when she showed him a confidentiality agreement that had been ratified between Woodbridge and Lilton that he established what supposedly lay behind the success of the commercial. She made enquiries on Mason's behalf, hoping to recruit an expert in neurophysiology who would understand what Lilton believed made SI work effectively. Unlike all previous attempts, Lilton was certain that human brain delta wave modulation of visual pictures made imprinting highly effective. It was all very convincing, but after Lilton's death there was no way at first to determine exactly how the delta wave modulation was imposed on visual information. After Mason interviewed Dr Nigel Armstrong (then at UCL)

Armstrong agreed to investigate the only known example of a working SI technique, that of the Autoclean commercial. This resulted in him recruiting in turn Simon Rogers (1998–2033, now deceased, lost in the Swiss Alps) then a post-graduate student at UCL with expertise in computer sciences and particularly video compression techniques. Between the two they established that the delta modulation was realized by moderately varying the brightness (the 'luminance') of a picture at a rate of between two to five cycles per second (the frequency of the human delta brainwave). At this time Mason asked that his head of CGI in the agency (Samuel Taylor CBE, now deceased, 1990–2054) be trained by Armstrong and Rogers to modulate the next chosen TV commercial. However, before this could happen representatives of the British National Union approached Mason and asked that Morley, Swan & Bramly produce their forthcoming electoral TV broadcasts. It appears that the BNU were prepared to pay an enormous sum in order to get Mason to apply the secret of the Autoclean commercial to their own programmes. It is now understood that the BNU sponsors were both financial and corporate heads who had been promised enormous tax concessions should the BNU triumph in the election.

Whatever the truth regarding the price the BNU were prepared to pay (and no figure has ever been confirmed, although it is known that considerable bonuses were paid to MS&B staff) Elliot Mason agreed to act for the BNU and had his staff start work on three electoral broadcasts, all three of which were to be transmitted over a ten-day period two weeks before the 2025 general election. It seems clear that each BNU programme was delta modulated and the broadcasts were transmitted as received from the agency.

From the material gleaned from Samuel Taylor's biographical notes prior to his death, it was Armstrong and Rogers who supervised and validated the SI in the BNU programmes that were broadcast before the election. Taylor was not included directly in the SI arrangement at that time. Armstrong and Rogers only gave him training in the essential SI technique immediately after they were involved with the BNU project.

After the election, both Armstrong and Rogers absented themselves from the agency until called for. Rogers in particular, because he was completing his PhD thesis at his home in Shropshire.

It is well known that the BNU received a landslide electoral outcome and thereafter began what has become known as the 'Fascist Interval' in British politics. Indeed, this time was so miserable a period for the nation that the onset of civil war was only prevented by the violently oppressive nature of the new government's security forces. The so-called 'public wardens', and large numbers of dutiful police officers, managed to suppress the outbreaks of public disorder, demonstrations and riots. These social upheavals occurred periodically, soon after the new administration took office and started to rule by decree.

It was Mason and his team who were once again approached by the BNU, this time to produce some public information (or propaganda) material to be broadcast to the nation over three nights. The programmes were to be approved by the party chiefs and officers at a showing in Westminster Hall. By this time Mason had become wholly disillusioned with the BNU and its party chiefs. He planned to dispose of the whole BNU administration once and for all by delta modulating the propaganda programmes and inserting notices in the video frames inviting the viewer to seek death (Taylor, personal diary). Nigel Armstrong suggested how this could be done in a video link from his retreat in the Orkney Islands. At the other end of the link, in the London office, were Elliot Mason and Samuel Taylor.

Armstrong suggested using the original SI technique. That was, to insert four virtually imperceptible death-appealing messages evenly spaced into the on-screen picture in conjunction with Lilton's delta modulation. Not knowing which message would have the greatest impact, he added that using all four at intervals in the visual picture over the whole length of the programme should have the desired effect. It was Taylor who prepared the programme DVDs to be shown to the BNU (Taylor, ibid). However, the BNU had stipulated that the screening of the preview be carried out with virgin versions, with no attempt to impose any 'augmentation' (i.e. delta SI. Taylor, ibid).

However, as Taylor has detailed elsewhere (*New Times* – 12/5/2048), Mason, with amazing composure and in the face of probable exposure, managed to exchange the virgin versions for a set that had been delta modulated and with the Armstrong messages inserted. The outcome was as expected; most of the senior administration and their officers were found dead over the next four days.

For a short time it appears, the remnants of the loathed administration managed to combat the almost immediate reaction to the deaths of most of the senior BNU politicians, particularly that of Feldt, the then prime minister. Street battles ensued with heavy casualties on both sides. Many street battles in London, Leeds and Bradford and other major towns were at first crushed, but the clashes between opponents of the BNU regime and security forces subsided for other reasons; not least the growing reluctance of the police and 'security forces' to mistreat, kill and alienate people for whom they had a high degree of empathy. When Nicholas Frobisher, the minister of finance and, after the executive deaths, the last surviving senior BNU politician, issued a proclamation imposing a daylight curfew and calling in the army, all demonstrations seemed to cease.

According to Taylor (personal discussion with Martin Naylor – *New Times* –12/5/2048), at this time Elliot Mason was subject to a death warrant issued by Frobisher who, because of the SI modulated programmes shown to the BNU executive at Westminster Hall, conveniently blamed Mason for the deaths of the prime minister and most of the BNU administration. This, as we now know, was entirely false. Unbeknown to Mason, he was actually a credible scape-goat for Frobisher, even though he himself was convinced that it was the SI-modulated programmes that had killed the executive and many others. Yet for all this he confessed to Taylor at the time (Taylor, ibid) that irrespective of his hand in 'mass murder' he had absolutely no regrets of any kind and felt vindicated. However, he was rightly concerned that Frobisher's threats were real, made the more intimidating by the fact that due to the street fighting he, and the agency staff, were trapped in the building where their offices were. He thought of himself as a sitting duck. If a hit squad or a sniper arrived outside the building, there was no easy escape.

The story of how Mason and Taylor escaped the agency building in Taylor's car, picked up some discarded weapons and drove to the gardens at the back of 10 Downing Street to assassinate Frobisher is now legend.

The truth however is stranger still, in that Frobisher was nowhere near Downing Street at the time, having flown to Sandringham to consult King Charles and his frail mother the Queen. Apparently, the army chiefs of staff, the police chief constables and all other senior military and civil servants had refused to comply with Frobisher's instructions on the basis that given the circumstances, they owed allegiance to the crown and not a self-proclaimed prime minister or a defunct government. Only the King, they insisted, could sanction any proclamation made by Frobisher. On advice, the King refused. Thwarted, Frobisher returned by helicopter to land at Horse Guards parade ground. Mason and Taylor, close at hand to the landing area (since the parade ground virtually abutted the Downing Street gardens) waited for the aircraft to land and then opened fire. Sir Elliot was once heard to remark that he and Taylor probably fired no more than ten to twelve rounds before the helicopter exploded, killing everyone on board and the one surviving bodyguard waiting by a car.

It seems that Sir Elliot made peace with his conscience after the death of Frobisher and foreswore ever involving himself in advertising again. He did however say that he might one day stand for Parliament, though for Taylor what kind of party Mason held allegiance to, or what kind of political campaign he might make, was speculative (Taylor, ibid).

As is well known, from 2035 Mason held the Bramwell seat for twenty-three years and ran as an independent, being politically unaffiliated.

Strange as it might seem, after picking up Mason's car at the agency building an hour after the Horse Guards fire fight, and after giving their farewells to each other, Taylor and Mason never met again.

There are of course some serious omissions and non-sequiturs in this story. Taylor later said that neither he nor Mason could explain why it was that, as they drove towards the Downing Street gardens, the whole of London appeared to be deserted. Hardly a soul was in evidence and, when a few people were seen, they quickly turned their backs or dived indoors. This was later explained as a case of peaceful demonstration – the populace of London had been asked by anti-government factions that when the army appeared they were not to provoke or engage them or refuse to obey the imposition of the Frobisher daylight curfew. That the army and civil police did not appear on the streets is explained above. When, on their return to Fleet Street, Mason and Taylor began to see more and more activity they put it down mainly to their delta modulated TV notice 'Don't obey any government edict or order' that Samuel Taylor had despatched to the operational TV channels before departing for Horse Guards. In this they were partially correct – the notice was sufficient in itself.

Of the many other anomalies in the tale, the one that usually puzzles is what caused the mass deaths of the executive after the BNU 'public information' programmes. If it wasn't Mason and SI, what was it? Enquiries and investigations a few years after restoration of the traditional democratic vote indicated that less than a third of the BNU senior officers actually died, and even then, other than Frobisher and his entourage, none by Elliot Mason's hand. Subsequent exhumation and post-mortem investigations demonstrated conclusively that at least the majority of deaths were caused by deadly force, there being some twenty-seven cases identified as execution style gunshots to the back of the head. This included Feldt, the prime minister. There is little doubt that this was the result of Frobisher's execution teams enacting a coup d'état by having all his rivals eliminated by clandestine executions. His expectations were however dashed by Mason and Taylor and the sullen resistance of the UK population.

That said, we must finally explore the controversial subject of subliminal imprinting.

We know that many people believed that SI associated with delta wave luminance modulation had a profound effect on a subject viewing a programme. This has never been entirely and absolutely discredited until two recent studies (allowed under a special government dispensation) were published. It is now clear that SI, of whatever form, does not work, and all those involved in this technique were seriously mistaken.

Emma Lilton's early research was insufficient to confirm conclusively that delta wave modulation had any profound effect. However, coupled to some tremendously successful applications (Autoclean/BNU/death messages and so on) there was no reason to believe it didn't.

It appears that in accordance with many earlier studies using simple SI (no delta wave modulation) the effect of SI is negligible (Stanley R. & Moors D. *British Jrn of Psychology* 5/2048/ pp 111–145) and that even with the addition of delta wave modulation the results are statistically insignificant (Morton D. *et al Jrn of Behavioural Sciences* 7/2047/ pp 203–241). At least three other reputable studies prior to the above (2005–2015) have shown that the effect of modulated SI is negligible and agree with the two studies cited here. In short, subliminal imprinting does not imprint anything!

Yet, it is said, how could the Autoclean advertisement have become so successful, and how could Mason have convinced the electorate to vote so overwhelmingly for the BNU?

If it wasn't the effect of SI, what was it?

It appears that the Autoclean success was founded on the fact that the commercial became very widely distributed; it appeared not just on UK television broadcasts but world-wide. At first, a number of international motoring magazines featured it as a new product and gave it their endorsement. Added to this was the very entertaining animation and covering music, which caused the commercial to go viral on the internet. As a result, sales and repeat of sales went global. It was an irrefutable case of secondary or parallel promotion, and not to do with SI.

As for the BNU, recent studies have formed the over-whelming conclusion that the reasoning inherent in the electoral programmes, and the unambiguous revealing of the then government's deficiencies, led many voters to cast a protest vote. In short, the BNU electoral programmes were so persuasive and credible that the electorate swung in the BNU's favour. No appreciable influence came from the delta modulation used on the luminance signal.

The consensus is that what marked Mason's work was his political insight and his highly impressive presentations, which left a viewer easily able to review their opinions and change their attitude to an issue. So convincing were the programmes under Mason's direction that there was little need to resort to SI or any delta modulation as originally proposed by Dr Emma Lilton. We conclude that had Jonathan Woodbridge turned down Emma Lilton's original proposal about SI then, regardless, the Autoclean advertisement would have been equally successful. Indeed, when Elliot Mason eventually succeeded Jonathan Woodbridge and grappled with the BNU electoral programmes, it is more than likely that the overall outcome would have been the same, in that the work of Mason and his teams was so discerning and of such high quality that the effect was indistinguishable from that of the same programme modulated with delta SI. Furthermore, the delta modulated TV message 'Don't obey any government edict or order' broadcast as Mason and Taylor went after Frobisher was assumed to have taken effect because of the delta modulation, but this cannot be true. The more plausible explanation is that it coincided with a decision by the underground opposition to comply with the message and stand firm.

It goes without saying that regardless of the reality regarding the use of SI so many years ago, its apparent consequences forced Sir Elliot into drastic action in order to remedy what he believed SI and his own hand had done to create an evil regime. Sir Elliot's enmity towards the BNU regime, and subsequently his malice towards Frobisher in particular, was predicated on his intrinsic sense of fairness coupled to an underlying burden of guilt, all of which provoked his actions. That he, along with Samuel Taylor, bravely removed a scourge from our nation has to be admired. It is inconsequential that he should take the blame for the installation of a thoroughly destructive and malevolent regime; once he had confronted his own apparent mistake, he undertook enormously risky steps to remedy it. That he did so without fear or compunction makes those of lesser courage stand in awe. The BNU Westminster Hall episode and the attack on Frobisher's helicopter stand as deeply courageous acts.

Sad it was that at the time he was ignorant of his misconceptions regarding SI. We might speculate that had he realized that he was not directly responsible through the use of SI for the Fascist Interval, he would not have done what he did. In one sense he was responsible for the Fascist Interval, but only because his keen political insight made their party political broadcasts so convincing. In the ensuing years he never accepted that SI was not a factor. In short, he divested himself of a culpability that did not really exist and he was not directly responsible for, though had he not misconstrued the power of SI and his entire role in the BNU rise to power, we would not now be free of it.

Sir Elliot's knighthood, conferred ten years after the events related above, was wholly justified. His death takes from us another hero; a hero we would all like to emulate if circumstances would allow it. Faced with the same quandary as Elliot Mason, would we risk our lives simply to settle a burning conscience?